MW01026597

WHAT YOU MAKE OF ME

WHAT YOU MAKE OF ME

A Novel

Sophie Madeline Dess

PENGUIN PRESS | NEW YORK | 2025

PENGUIN PRESS
An imprint of Penguin Random House LLC
penguinrandomhouse.com

Designed by Nerylsa Dijol

LIBRARY OF CONGRESS CATALOGING-IN-PUBLICATION DATA
Names: Dess, Sophie Madeline, author.
Title: What you make of me : a novel / Sophie Madeline Dess.
Description: New York : Penguin Press, 2025. |
Summary: "A novel following two fiercely competitive and co-dependent siblings whose desires as artists, thinkers, and lovers come to a head when they fall for the same woman, forcing them to confront not only their precarious relationship with each other, but what it means to sacrifice for the sake of art" —Provided by publisher.
Identifiers: LCCN 2024013327 (print) | LCCN 2024013328 (ebook) |
ISBN 9780593830826 (hardcover) | ISBN 9780593830833 (ebook)
Subjects: LCGFT: Novels.
Classification: LCC PS3604.E7636 W47 2025 (print) |
LCC PS3604.E7636 (ebook) | DDC 813/.6—dc23/eng/20240513
LC record available at https://lccn.loc.gov/2024013327
LC ebook record available at https://lccn.loc.gov/2024013328

Printed in the United States of America
1st Printing

For my grandfather

WHAT YOU MAKE OF ME

In two weeks they'll be killing my brother and so I'm writing. I shouldn't be. My brother would agree with me. Writing is not my art.

I am a painter, though I don't expect you to have heard of me. If you saw me at a café you would not know me. You'd have no questions for me. Soft pop would be thumping and you'd be into it, and I'd only be another person sitting there plain-faced with blueberry eyes, my hair dyed some variation of oat or vanilla, shirt and pants bleeding together in one wheaty monochrome.

If I were to look at *you* as you stood there ordering, I'd wonder all the questions one asks when faced with a stranger, like who you sleep with, and how, and what you think of before bed, and what it would be like to press my nose into your scalp. But neither of us is at the café. I am here working, writing. My first solo show is coming up at a small gallery called Withheld. The Withheld people recently called me to say they were going to send their assistant up to my apartment to look at all my work, so that she might write some flap copy. Fine. But then I heard that this flap copy was supposed to describe exactly what my paintings "do" and what they "mean." These explanations were to be printed on a single sheet of paper. This sheet of paper—trifolded—would be called the "catalog." And this little catalog would be printed a hundred times over and would sit stacked on a plastic tray at the front of the gallery, available to gallery-goers upon entry or exit.

For days they've been sending her to my door, the assistant. For days she's been knocking at noon and for days I have denied her entry. (Under any other circumstances I'd have allowed her in. She is chatty and structurally perfect. Her face in particular, because of its modernity and slight resemblance to a kitchen, has an industrial beauty. Vast cheeks. Boxy nose.) If she came in now she'd see me naked, perched here on my small metal stool. I've just opened the window. A gently polluted breeze is sifting off the sidewalk and I'm spreading my legs, letting the air come up cool through my crotch and hot out my mouth. I make it work like an organ sweep, a little urban exorcism. The only stimulants in this whole space are my paintings, placed like mistakes along my wall.

All the paintings are of my brother. You would not recognize him in them. In real life my brother has a straight line down his nose, caramel hair that waves upward, and eyes that are a very difficult blue like there's black beneath them. But in the paintings you won't find him like this. I've given him new shapes. You might mistake his cheek for an elephant tusk. His mouth for a small vat of blood. His nose the cracked edge of a tile.

What I mean to say is, Withheld will not be trifolding me and my dying brother into that little catalog. I'll do it myself. All this time I've been sitting up here feeling dramatic, feeling nothing, thinking: *That lucky boy gets to drop off and I'm stuck here clinging.* Now, however, I'm starting to feel the holy series of convictions one must always feel when setting out on something new: *This is the best idea I've ever had; this is the only idea I've ever had; this is the only idea anyone has ever had.* I'm aware these convictions sound less exciting when written. That's always the way with language, an insufficient medium. I try not to use or consume it. It's not that I haven't read, it's that I'm an adolescent reader. I read too selfishly. I pick up books trying to figure out more about myself—as my brother, Demetri, has advised. The issue is that the reading turns me into other people whom I soon after abandon. And this reminds me that for the most part the self is only something that continually takes up, plays with, and then abandons other selves. I don't need to be reminded of this. And, anyway, words should be spoken, not written. Like how they used to do it—a return to the glory days of oral!

As I am now understanding, the worst thing about

writing is that it takes time. Therefore writers must believe in old-fashioned things like focus. I have no faith in this. My faith is in the image, in instantaneity, in the ability to see and say it all at once.

In a sense Demetri's faith was also in the image. He worked in documentaries. His most recent piece, unfortunately, is a film (or documentary, even though it contains no official documents, it only wants to *constitute* a document in itself, which I refuse to concede that it does), a film about us, mostly about me, but not too much on this because it embarrasses me, and I will only say that when I found out he made it, at first I really thought: good. That's fine. At least it's off his chest. In fact I was surprised he got it done. Because often my brother was the victim (Is the victim? What's the tense for the dying?) of what he only semi-ironically called his spiritual quests. The specifics of these quests are irrelevant, just know he was one of those people whose life centered around moral questions like am I wrong, did I do wrong, how can I amend?

Demetri would sit naked in the East Tenth Street bathhouses and think about these questions. He'd sweat them out.* He'd run to the bodega for a bag of Smartfood and a

---

****Out***, oil on linen, 40 × 50 cm, medium
I'm listing the dimensions in centimeters and realizing it's going to be very hard to picture the "sizes" of canvases in your head. What regular person knows what 40 × 50 cm really looks like? Those numbers are for buyers who know the dimensions of the blank space on their wall where they want to put something, not for people who want to actually imagine.

tub of mouthwash and come back empty-handed, the questions having distracted him. He believed that the only way to get at them was to privately and deliberately dedicate his life to them. His making the film—the *documentary*—was a way to come to some answers. Still, I found out he made it and thought: No one will care. No one will watch it. I forgave him. I went to his sickbed, looked into his sunken, radiating face and I said: "This is pretty good revenge for my having oppressed you, Demetri. And so I forgive you." But it's true I'm having a bit of trouble forgiving myself.

Nati and I were on the phone recently, and with her typical coldness she said I was the one who killed Demetri. "You're the reason he'll die." Not that you care about her yet, but I'd like you to know that that's the kind of person we're dealing with. Alas.

They'll really kill him now (though they like to say they're *letting him go*, releasing him—which is to say, restricting him from air and feed). It's happening in two weeks at 3:00 p.m. By some accounts—those of certain doctors or philosophers—he is already dead. He has what is called a depressed consciousness. A tumor is sitting squat on his meninges. And now his brain stem has turned inward, become a stubborn child with its arms crossed, refusing to liaison properly between the spinal cord and cerebrum.

Still, as he dies his pride only seems to grow. I go to his little sickroom to visit him. He's arranged it so that the Replacements and Pharoah Sanders are playing through his speakers on rotation. He is lying in bed, silent. His face stares up at nothing and is dry, glowing. His smile—which I'm always reminded is not actually a smile, only an involuntary twitch of the zygomaticus minor—has been suggesting all these very bad jokes which are all really true. I wish I could think of one now. I'll have my own when I die. I know this because the nurse told me, with her scrub authority, that death is always attended by bad jokes and basic truths, unlike life where everyone's hilarious and lying all the time. She was serious.

Anyway, he is there, and soon the doctors will enter his room, and they will call me, and I will stay here, writing.

One last thought about writing. I'm thinking: If I were to tell you I was painting your portrait so that I'd capture everything you are and everything you've ever been—just by looking at you for hours at a time—you would be excited, you would be eager to *see where I took it.* But if I were to tell you I was *writing* the story of your life, using hard facts and descriptions, you might feel trapped. You might feel a more literal transcription of your life would have nothing to do with what is real to you. It would not capture the unknowable bits of you (the way a painting could). That's all I mean, that writing—with all its specifics—has a harder time with the real. This consistent loss of faith in reality becomes (for me) a problem that extends beyond language. For instance, my suspicion of my own life is deepest when I think I might be feeling something "real," like when I think I might be in love, or when I think I've at last succeeded, or even when I think I might've failed but in a rich way—any time when I know some deep sense of meaning should be tunneling into the soul somewhere, but is not. I lose faith. Anyway . . .

Demetri's film about us: I haven't seen it and don't plan to. I didn't ask him for details about it. I didn't ask if there were close-ups of my eyes or my teeth. If everyone was going to see the way they're gnarled into my gums and come out in this stacked and slanted kind of way. I didn't ask for a plot summary (of my own life!) or for structural details. I can guess at the outline. Demetri will start when we are children.

He was obsessed with youth, and with posterity. In fact before he really began dying he convinced me to donate a painting of mine to our high school. This was after I started making a bit of money. I'd sold a couple pieces at auction. I'd been written about and reviewed (I'd been called a "force" but it was still "unclear" if I was worth being reckoned with; I'd been called "powerful" but they didn't know if the watercolor of me being railed from behind was "liberative" for women or if it only "reaffirmed submission"). A donation at that point, three years ago, would be a small asset for the school district. "Donate them an old one, a good one," Demetri instructed me. He was so insistent, I came to understand, because he wanted the chance to go speak to the school—in Longhead, Long Island, a tiny town you don't know and don't want to—he wanted to go back there and lecture. By then that was what he did for me. He'd come up with things to say about my work, to flick it spinning into the world and give it direction. We wouldn't consult about what he wrote. He wouldn't ask me if he got my work "right" and I wouldn't ask him to be sure to include this or that. We never discussed whether his written copy or my actual art was what got me into certain shows, galleries, homes.

The school was happy to have him visit. They were excited about his return. There's even a recording of the talk he gave. I often find myself pulling up the video and watching him. The way he stands recklessly tall at the little podium. I watch his face twitch around before the young crowd settles. He does not know what to say to teenagers. He's prepared a speech, but at the last moment he has scrapped it. Now he stands there and clears his throat until it sores. He tells the room full of pubescents that in order to calm down he's going to imagine them naked. He blushes and rapidly takes this back. And then says it again. He asks how many of them have any grandparents left. He says he is there to discuss a trip to the Virgin Islands and then asks how many people have been to an island or know of a virgin. He cannot settle down.

"Ava and I were taken to a Virgin Island, once. It was our first flight," he finally begins. "I was nine. Ava was eight. On the plane we were sitting twenty rows away from our father. Because we were loud, in the way that tragedies can make you really rambunctious." He coughs. "On the plane"—he tilts forward, toward the mic—"I grew bored. I began taking hold of little threads of Ava's hair and gnashing them between my teeth," he tells them. "When she felt the tug she turned, saw a chunk of her hair in my mouth, my eyes wide. We both burst out. Ava had a way of shrieking when she laughed, she kind of threw her head back and bore all her teeth. Back then her canines were just coming in, breaking out through the pulp, which made her look ferocious. So we really just sat there and shrieked, smacked each other, leapt up in our seats." He explains to the children that I fell in love on this trip. "When the flight attendant came to quiet us, Ava told him she thought he was beautiful, and that he had beautiful eyes. She thought it was good form to let a person know." Here Demetri stalls. The light thins his body and for a moment he stands there shrinking.*

In his speech Demetri skips over much of the vacation. He picks things up at the end. But the trip itself was an eternity.

We landed on the island and were shepherded into a van that would immediately take us to the hotel, as if to look or go elsewhere were criminal. In the van Demetri and my

---

**Shrinking*, oil on linen, medium
How to capture enthusiasm in the shrinking shadow of a malnourished body? Use extra oil. Let it wrinkle.

father sat across from me, arm to arm. The van went over a bump; everyone was for a moment lifted out of their seats, except for our father, who did not lift. I watched his profile—his nose a blade slicing through the blur of trees. Our father reminded us where we were and asked if we remembered anything about colonialism. Demetri did.

At the hotel our father spoke with the suited and sweating men behind the desk. Demetri and I left him. We stood out on the lobby's balcony and looked into the ocean. We'd been promised clear ocean water, but all we saw was black, with bursts of bright navy far out where the sun hit. "You're mad," Demetri said to me, "because the water's not see-through, and because you were in love with the flight attendant, and he didn't love you back."

I considered this. "You're mad," I said.

"About?"

"Excretions." We'd heard the term on the plane, from two vagina doctors on holiday.

Demetri turned to me: "You are largely vaginal."

"You are a vagina."

We heard a woman come out onto the balcony and stand behind us. She asked if we were admiring the view.

"No," Demetri said. He looked at me—we conspired not to turn toward her. "I wouldn't say that we're admiring the view."

The woman laughed. She seemed impressed with her own laughter, with her very ability to laugh, especially with children. "Not admiring the view? What are you doing then?"

Demetri considered this. "Observing it," he said.

"That's hilarious," the woman said. When I turned toward her, she smiled. Her teeth were pulled tight together, so bright that they seemed to make noise. She edged toward us.

"Are you two here alone? No parents?" she asked. We felt her smile continue behind our backs. I began to answer, but Demetri spoke first.

"Just our father is here," he said. I didn't think he was going to say it. "Because our mother is in the ocean. She ran in last year."

The woman was not sure now. We waited for her. She looked at me. We'd seen this look before, from all the town mothers. The pity and distaste whenever Demetri and I were frank about death—their concern over whether or not to believe us, their wondering if we had not inherited the melodrama, or if indifference was its alternative form. The woman paused. "Honey"—she looked down toward me—"is that true?"

I looked at Demetri, who kept himself busy by pretending to notice something in the trees.

"No," I said. I tried to take up Demetri's method: "Our mother did not run. She walked into it very slowly." This was true. Our mother was an actress. She had started off in Shakespeare and ended up in commercials. On the night of her death she took the tripod out onto the porch and recorded herself walking into the Sound—a recording that Demetri did not watch but that he often watched me watch, until it was taken from me. Anyway, this trip was our time to recalibrate, as we heard it described. It was our reintroduction to the water. It was important to start where the water was clear, where you could see all the way through to the bottom—except that we could not.

On the porch Demetri and I had the sudden urge to get rid of this woman. "Ava," he shouted, and pointed toward a nearby branch. A thick green fluid was developing at the end of a leaf. I didn't know what he was going to say but I primed myself for action. Before we could perform, our father stepped outside. A room key in his breast pocket.

"Okay," he said to us.

The woman smiled and took a step back.

"Sorry," our father said.

Since she possessed an extreme, conventional beauty I watched to see how he looked at her but there was nothing in his face.

She suggested he really need not apologize and stepped toward him, offering him her hand. "Édith," she said, "I'm the resident artist here. I paint portraits of families on the beach, usually at sunrise and sunset, if you are ever interested." She pointed out a small bungalow to the right of the greeting center. "That's my studio. If you three would like a quick tour . . ." She looked at Demetri and me. It was clear that she expected our excitement. We stayed quiet. She looked again at our father.

"It's nice to meet you," he said.

"It's nice to meet you," I echoed. Demetri reached out and hooked his arms around our father's legs. "It's nice to meet you," he said, echoing us.

Édith smiled halfway, like she'd made a mistake that eluded her.

Demetri and I left our father, who took our bags. Alone, we made our way to the pool: it was unguarded, empty. We stripped to our underwear and got in. Demetri was desperate to conduct the laugh test. "It's because," he told me, bobbing, "when you laugh your muscles relax and you breathe out really hard and you can't swim anymore." He was clumsy in the water. His wet hair in a jagged rim around his head like an inverted crown. "And so you drown and die," he explained.

"So test it," I said.

He dunked his head into the water and then sprang up high, his eyes crossed, and shouted, "FUCK your DICK." He yelled it as he leapt, his arms straight by his sides. "ANAL."

I nearly burst. I bared my teeth and kicked out into the water, springing away. I managed to scream his name. I was still laughing as I sank. Demetri watched as water began to funnel through my mouth. I thrust my neck back for air and looked at the sky, a bruised, mean blue with small scraps of cloud. I called his name again. He didn't come for me, but I didn't drown. Soon we collected ourselves. We climbed out and sat on the ledge with our legs still in the water. For a number of minutes we stayed silent.

"Do my eyes look like yours right now?" I asked, turning to him. His eyes were wide open.

"I don't know, how do mine look?"

"Blue," I said, "but with sun stuck in the blue." I looked closer into his color. "A sticky blue."

He put his head closer to mine—focusing on my left eye, then my right. "No, I don't think so."

I told him his breath smelled like clay—which it did, and which it does still. Even now his sickroom has the stench of sediment.

Soon we heard footsteps behind us, and when we turned we recognized Édith—she had taken off her hat. I remember her auburn hair matched her reddish eyes exactly, but only because I felt Demetri notice this beside me. He had stopped breathing.

"Are you two hollering?" Édith asked us, her hands laced together and pressed against her stomach.

"You paint portraits," I said to her, standing up. Demetri followed. "So do I."

Édith smiled with the same sympathy as before. We wanted to tell her not to. "I do, yes. And that's very nice," Édith said, nodding and smiling anyway. "It's always good to paint. To have a variety of hobbies, especially at such a young age." She nodded and nodded. Even back then I must've thought some variation of, This person only drinks wine.

Demetri and I stood together, looking very portraitable, we must've thought. We waited for Édith's offer to paint us right then. Instead she stood in silence. My hair was wet. I felt it sticking to my neck, in plaits over my shoulders. I knew my stomach was out, hard and bloated. I felt my legs glued together. I waited for Édith. Édith said nothing.

"You have a good dress on," I said to her.

Édith looked down at her dress. It was white linen, with a tan belt tight around her ribs. "Thank you." She smiled.

Together Demetri and I waited, again, for our invitation to be painted. But Édith only stared, as if requesting that we go on speaking. Just when I had come up with something, Demetri bolted—for such a small body his wet feet slapped heavy against the cement. I waited a minute to try to let Édith talk to me some more. She failed. I ran back to the bungalow.

Demetri had not yet gone in. He was there standing by the door, his finger to his lips. "Shh," he said. "He's sleeping." He meant our father. "He's going to sleep all day."

We sat on the ground outside the door. The stone's grain sharpened into my ankles. Demetri let insects crawl onto his finger, then shepherded them onto his palm—ants, small spiders. "COLONIZE ME," he yelled at them.

The sun was still high. It had taken on a sourness.

Demetri kept spitting. Sitting there doing nothing we began to sweat.

"Okay," I said, standing.

"We need hard hats," Demetri said as we marched down to the beach, making our way by what Demetri thought an adult might call a charmingly ramshackle footpath. "We can melt these rocks."

I told him we needed to go missing.

"That would be relaxing." He asked me if I had known our father would be sleeping the whole time.

I said no. Our father slept all day at home, too, but we thought it was because our house was dark, exhausting. The island, however, was not. As we walked, I felt my face burning. I scratched my skin like this would scrape off the heat. We continued in silence until the branches cleared and the first hint of water was visible. We heard lapping before we saw the waves, at which point I screamed Demetri's name and raced toward the shore, running all the way to the edge. There, I looked out. The water at last was clear and bright, pulled tight under the sun. I turned to find Demetri, who had stopped between the bushes and the shoreline, and waved at him to come. He didn't move. I called him over twice more and assured him you could see all the way down through the water, into the sand. When he still didn't come, I turned back toward him.

We stood watching the waves. I started telling Demetri how it smelled like salt and moss and water, and he told me

I was wrong and that those were just objects and not scents, which were different categories of thought, even though he knew objects could have scents, but back then he was stuck in the habit of trying to give order to things because he thought it might give him power, and thought without power was useless. And just as he was asking me to describe the scent of salt—just to see if I could—we caught sight of Édith. She was standing farther down the beach, with her dress bellying out behind her, painting a family posed before the sunset.

I turned to Demetri and braced myself. "Do you think I'm beautiful?" I asked him.

He pretended not to hear me. "Where?"

"Do you think that I am beautiful?"

"I don't know what you mean," he said.

I told him never mind. We looked again toward the water.

"No," he answered.

"Okay."

"When you laugh, maybe," he said.

So I laughed.

"No, not then, either."

I laughed harder.

"Sorry," he said.

I looked down the beach, toward Édith.

This is where, in his speech, Demetri picks it up: "Ava thought it was good form not just to tell a person they were beautiful but to do something about it. And so on our second morning on the island, before the sun was even up, I pretended to be sleeping when I heard her leave our room. She was gone for maybe an hour or two. When she came back I kept my eyes closed. I didn't want to know. But soon she was standing over me and letting liquid drip off her body and onto my arm. She whispered my name." He whispers his own name into the mic. "So this is it, I lay there thinking. Ava and I were always waiting for 'the bad thing,' the bad thing that would end all other bad things, and I thought, *This* is going to be the bad thing. Ava whispered to me she was going to turn on the lamp. She did. I looked at her. In the lamplight I thought someone had torn her open. She was covered in blues and pinks and reds. It looked like one giant organ had exploded—like she was turned inside out, dying." Here Demetri pauses for dramatic effect, and then:

"'I ruined them,' Ava explained to me there in our room.

"'Your clothes?' I asked her.

"She didn't answer.

"'What did you ruin?'"

Demetri tells his audience that I had entered Édith's studio by the window and had not only ruined her paintings but left her with one of my own, a portrait of a man whom no one else would recognize, but who Demetri and I knew as the flight attendant, painted in my clumsy green strokes overlaid with a loose, watery white, whose sheeny effect was ruined when the paints mixed, as I did not give the green its time to dry.

Back then the trouble we got into was constant, and as such irrelevant to us, and so when we were kicked out of the hotel—off the island, effectively—the only thing that mattered was that the hotel manager, after informing us of our forced departure, did not suggest that I throw out my work. He looked me in the eye as he returned it to me. "And I assume you want this back," he had said. I nodded yes and took it from him. Again he looked at me with a sense of solemnity, as if we had agreed on something and that that something was to do with the rest of my life. I carried the portrait with me through the airport. It was something sacred and dangerous—I would not let it go. It was too large to take onto the plane. They were going to make us check it. Our father wanted to throw it out. I refused. "Leave it here," he warned me. I didn't listen. He walked away from us after yelling obscenities at the airport floor. That was the only moment of brief rupture (and it wasn't necessarily between us, but within him). Otherwise he frightened everyone by staying extraordinarily calm.

"This is the portrait we'll be donating," Demetri tells the auditorium. From the audience there is a chorus of *ohs*. "And the point is"—he finds refuge in this phrase—"the point is Ava had told Édith that she, Ava, was also a painter. And Édith had said it was always good to have a hobby. But! When someone calls what is necessary for you a *hobby*—as if it is a trivial reprieve, you know, a rest, a break from an arduous life and not the arduous life itself—they are trying to control you. Remember that worse than an inability to fulfill a desire is to have no real desire at all. There are people like this in the world. They will confuse you. They will want to control you. Refuse to be controlled."

I groan every time. You righteous fuck, I want to say to him. These kids are already refusing control. The nature of the child is refusal. Although, maybe, who knows. Maybe they are at the age when the mind gets co-opted. They are in that season of damage when curiosity gets frosted over by the cool of disinterest. If that's the case, Demetri's body here is convincing. It is enough to keep them present. His right hand is on the podium, his left arm is up in the air, fingers stretched wide. He leans from side to side in a rare shamanic death dance. His hair's thinning. The tumor was formed by then and it makes him giddy, and the students like his energy. He's having fun. He's riding out the perimeter of existence.

I wonder if the young audience could tell he was dying. I'd say that maybe after Demetri stepped down from the podium, they ceased to think of him at all—that he came and spoke and was forgotten—but this would be impossible. You had to think things about him, even if only out of combativeness, because you knew he was standing there impressed by you in some way. His impressions of others were varied and inaccurate, and immovable once formed. Sometimes you could see yourself crystallizing* on his face. I bet at least a few of the students thought: This random man who smacks of decay is going to remember me. He better take this vision of me with him down to death, so at least when I arrive, a part of me is there already.

To give others the impression that they are unforgettable—that is grace. Sometimes my brother had it.

**Crystallizing*, oil with crushed glass on linen, medium
For the crushed glass I smashed a champagne flute, then ground the shards using a mortar and pestle we bought in Italy. Took forever. There is still a tiny glass shard stuck in my thumb and I can sometimes feel it pulsing like a little organ inside me.

On the rare occasion that I leave my apartment, I like to go where Demetri knew people and thought about them. I go to his supermarkets. His parks. His bars.

I think of him sitting in one—a bar called Bar Down—after we first moved to New York. I am twenty-one. Demetri is twenty-two. Everything is new to us, especially the bit of money I've just begun to make. Demetri is sitting on a stool wearing a dark red sweater, a leather vest on top. His hair is unbrushed and high on his head and he is riddled with that rootless* anxiety.

When I sit down, he starts telling me about the bartender: "She's in the bathroom right now but she's a very Ukrainian woman who speaks with a hot lisp and who lives an hour away in Red Hook. Her landlord is an obese Croat who lives above her and stomps his feet when he's

---

**Rootless*, smoke and soot on canvas, small-medium
To form an image with smoke, you simply hold a candle very close to the canvas for long periods of time until the surface begins to degrade in ways that please you.

jerking off and finishing, three times a day, but he apologizes to her, and when you look at her you'll see she actually likes it, thinks it's very New York because she's new here and loves it like that. I told her we were also kind of new here—"

I cut him off. That day I'm there to tell him about a new idea for a series of paintings called *LiveStreaming*. The idea is to set up an easel next to my bed, have sex with men, and paint in watercolor as they enter me—in fact I'd try to focus on painting the entire time that they were inside me and would paint the colors of the experience, letting wetted pigments stream together down the canvas. "Do you see?" I ask him. "Watercolor, an old-fashioned medium . . . intimate . . . but a modern exposure . . . a modern title . . ."

Demetri looks at me, eyes bright and cynical. "That's too easy, Ava," he says.

"It will actually be extremely difficult."

He tells me it feels cheap and that we can't afford to do anything that feels so cheap.

"It's just name building." I ask him if he knows how many musicians lose money on tour. I ask him if he knows that they expect to lose this money. They plan for it. The point is exposure.

Demetri smiles—his favorite way of saying no.

(I do the series anyway. The entire collection—five pieces, painted on eighteen-by-twenty-four-inch canvases—

was bought at once, marking my first major sell. It goes to an Armenian at auction. When we get the news that it has sold, Demetri doesn't mention his initial opposition. He goes on to speak on its behalf. And then, two months later, when the Armenian sells the pieces for three times what he paid, when we see none of this second-sale money, Demetri writes his essay on the immorality of the art market, in which he joins the chorus demanding artists get a healthy share of subsequent sales of their work. He writes with a frivolous person's ferocity. He's brought onto panels. On which he is filmed sitting, nervous, alert, convincing.)

At Bar Down—as he's telling me not to do it, not to paint the series—I don't answer him. It's because as he's speaking I see my mother. I register her with a benign sense of familiarity because this happens sometimes. She is there in the set of Demetri's jaw. She is in the way he moves his hand—in all the fleeting gestures, like the control center for his body is somewhere outside himself. Though I'll admit that on my mother everything was exaggerated. Her movements. Her expressions. Her lips and eyes took up far more facial space, giving her a surreality. You had to pay her keen attention. You had to be wary. Surreal people can coerce you into their excess.

She did this with us. Mostly with Demetri. With her he was agreeable: ready to be scooped up and taken into her car, into the nail salon, to the café, the bank, ready to ride the cart through Kroger. Ready to be in a room with her for hours, ready to hear me pacing outside the door, waiting, never asking. I, on the other hand, was indifferent, at times fearful of her, thinking: Don't look at me, because I will not impress you, and we'll both be angry about it.

On one rare occasion, Demetri asked without words if I could help him—if together we might control a certain situation: Demetri was going to be shipped away. This was before the island trip. Before our mother's trip into the Sound. Dr. Udolph, our principal, was coming to our house for dinner. Udolph sometimes doubled as French teacher, and it was in this capacity that she saw firsthand the supposed precocity of Demetri's shyness. She wanted to discuss the possibility of transferring him to a school upstate, where they'd tease out his timidity and make it productive.

We were new to Udolph's school. We'd been kicked out just the year before from another school, where we'd been happy until they called me oversexed because I thought I might learn a bit more about the organs within my pelvis. On my desk, pants down and legs spread open, I had my fellow first graders describe what they saw end to end. I had them launch fingers up the holes so we might see where-all it went. (I was only curious. And yet writing this I realize that their use of "oversexed" might have turned into a self-prophetic journey.) Demetri didn't cry when they decided to kick the both of us out, thinking we must be one and the same. He didn't wonder about what I'd done.

When we first arrived at the school, Udolph welcomed

us personally. She invited us into her office. She shook our hands and looked us in the eye.

And now, up on the stairs of our own home, waiting for her arrival, we both stared down at our mother. She wandered around the kitchen like it was some unknown range. She had changed into a gray satin gown for the occasion. She'd placed a sheer blue scarf over her shoulders. I recognized the scarf from an old photo of her starring as Nora in *A Doll's House*—in the photo it is whipped in defiance behind her. Down in the kitchen it was ruffled around her neck. Her steps were loud as she placed two large fish-shaped trays on the counter and then covered them with pigs in a blanket, crab puffs, two hard cheeses. For dinner she was making pasta with clams, to which she'd later add broccoli, which came in a bag, ready to be microwaved just before the meal.

Our father helped her set the bar: a bottle of brown liquor, and then, in a row along the counter, three short, heavy-bottomed crystal glasses. Demetri had recently broken the fourth glass while trying to balance it on his head.

As our mother paced, our father sat down and opened the newspaper, his favorite thing to pretend to read while he attentively watched her. Their sounds stretched up to us at the top of the stairs: the feigned turning of pages, the running sink, the sound of plate on plate. Finally the ticking, then the sharp, brief wind of the stove switched on, followed by a mild propane tang. Our mother leaned over the stove to watch the water boil (Demetri, all his life, would lean the same way, never letting water boil without watching it), and our father appeared to really read, and things fell silent. Up on the stairs Demi and I turned to each other. I pulled a hair band off my wrist and made a web of it with my fingers, whose pattern told us Demetri would have three wives. He looked scared. "Ava! You'll have to take one."

At last we were called into the kitchen. Earlier that evening we'd been instructed to wear nice clothing. For me it was my father's shirt, which had a collar and fell loose around my bare knees. Demetri wore a white drugstore T-shirt that looked nicer than it was because he'd just ripped it out of the packaging. "My pants?" he had asked me as we dressed. I threw him a skirt from my pile of clothing. It was pink with crystal studs in spiral patterns across the front and back. Demetri put it on. Thus attired, we strode toward our chairs. Our father sat up. It was rare, but in certain moments our father forgot himself and smiled without self-congratulation or defensiveness, or really any awareness at all, only pure pleasure at being amused. It was Demetri's favorite look—there was a closed circuit between them, and the current between them sent me the long way around the table.

Our mother sighed. She put her elbows up by her plate, weaved her fingers together and settled her chin upon them. Her eyes were a clear green—fastened hard on the wall clock. I turned around. Though I could not read analog, I understood it was time.

Demetri and I did not rise. Only when Udolph was indeed able to fit through our front door—I was the one who said it might be a problem—did Demetri look at me. Udolph, like me, was wide. I watched her turn under our foyer light, her freckles spread soft across her chest. She had tiny hair clips scattered slapdash around her wide-brimmed head, each cluttered with tiny fake pearls. Earrings pulled at her lobes. She smelled like sugar and limes. Demetri and I had heard her described as having a *queenly* gravity, but all the queens I could think of were stiff, old. Udolph was older, but if she had been painted by a master she'd look vital—when she smiled her wrinkles collected in tight, ruddy folds, wet light catching on her chin.

"Well, hello!" she said through the foyer.

Our father stood up but did not look at Udolph. He looked at our mother, who also did not look at Udolph but at the counter where all of the items were set up, because organized objects can stand in for sociability. Dr. Udolph adjusted quickly. She hung up her own coat, and then focused on whatever ambiance she felt she'd stepped into. She directed most of her attention to Demetri and me, quizzing us with state capitals and the names of the largest rivers in various parts of the country. Demetri's answers came out first and were more correct, but my voice was louder. Udolph considered it a tie.

When we sat to eat, our mother at last began to speak, with great deliberation, about the benefits that she hoped were a product of microwaved vegetables.

"Oh, completely," Dr. Udolph said. "I love my micro." She gave my mother a long look, as if after this agreement they might find their footing.

Instead, I was reminded that when a throat is cleared in silence, you can hear every drop of mucus bubbling up from the pharynx into the mouth and nose. You can see the mucus pooling in the cheeks, you can sense when it is swallowed. We kept waiting for Udolph to talk but this was all we heard.

Until Demetri turned to me: "It's supposed to be a full moon tonight."

"A full moon blinds you," I reminded him.

"Is that true?" Udolph asked me.

"It doesn't blind you," Demetri told me. "It gets into your eye. So there are little moons in the black part of every eye. How it's in your eyes, now."

"Really?" I sat up in my chair and looked at everyone one by one. My father looked at me and then looked away. My mother did not look. Dr. Udolph held my stare and started laughing.

"Demetri," our father said with his fork, "that is just the reflection of artificial light in the pupil. Not the moon."

"In a way," I conjectured, "all light is moonlight, because if it were not for the moon there would not be an earth"—I had just learned this—"and if there were not an earth there would not be light in eyes." She, too, excels, I thought they might be thinking. She, too, might be good enough to dispose of.

"Ave, that drains things of their immediate meanings—and their remote meanings," our father said. "The moon's light is more remote from us than you think, Demetri, by the way. For instance, it takes about a second and a quarter for the moon's light to reach us here on earth. And of course you know it's not really the moon's light at all, but the sun's light reflected off the moon."

"Well." Dr. Udolph leaned forward. She told us there would be very bright moons at the École Saratoga, and then leaned back again. "My sister runs the place, you know, for gifted children." She flashed Demi and me a warning look that was somehow still full of merriment. I tried to imagine her angry. She is childless, I remembered. "Especially rare to receive scholarships, as you understand. But if a recommendation comes from me, maybe there are avenues, there are roads."

"Highways," Demetri said, looking at me. "Tunnels."

"That's fantastic." Our father sat back. He looked at Demetri like *Do you know what might be happening to you?*

In the next phase of silence, I felt a vibration up my legs. Someone was tapping their foot against the floor. In the same moment I noticed our mother was sitting there, shaking, emitting hard waves of yellow light. “Well, I’ve been giving this a lot of consideration,” she said at last.

“Okay,” our father said, smiling and chewing too hard.

“Well,” our mother began. “France’s Napoleon the Great had a mother who would not attend his coronation. Did you know this?”

Dr. Udolph shook her head. Demetri’s eyes fell on me. We knew by then when our mother had prepared to say something that she had written down. In her dresser she kept a series of note cards. I knew this because when she and Demetri left the house I’d tear around her room. When I first found and read them I thought they were part of a diary, or a collection of memories, or lines from old plays, or upcoming commercials. Over time I understood I was reading the role she intended to play in conversations that she intended to have. I took a few cards with me into her bathroom. I studied them. I acted them to myself in the mirror. Soon I had them memorized. The next time she sat me down to explain why I must respect my father, why I must be kinder to him, why I must understand his weaknesses, I mouthed parts of her speech as she recited it to me. It was the one and only time I was slapped.

At the table I watched Udolph make patterns with her pasta as she waited for our mother to continue about Napoleon, about his mother.

“I only mean,” our mother said, “that in the painting his mother is right there in the center, even though she was not there at all. I only mean . . . that you cannot understate the influence . . ." But then our mother shook her head and did not go on.

"Are there art classes at Saratoga?" Demetri asked.

"Yes," I seconded, "is there a Mr. Sprigg?" I knew there could not be a Mr. Sprigg. He taught art at our school and was narrow, blue-faced, and quiet, with long, thin hair. In class he'd give us an assignment and then would spend the rest of the session tracing his hands with a light-toned pencil. He showed us endless paintings by Edvard Munch, which he hung around the classroom as if they were his own.

"There's not a Mr. Sprigg," Udolph answered. "But there are of course art classes. A pottery wheel. They also have woodworking. Are you two fond of Mr. Sprigg?"

"Not exactly," I said. This wasn't true, but I had already established my standards. "He seems embarrassed."

Udolph leaned in so far that her bosom pressed against her shirt. I stared into the freckled crevice. "And why's that?"

"He's just always embarrassed."

"You don't like him?" our father asked, surprised, as if Demi and I had spent all our days praising Mr. Sprigg and were only now being critical; as if he himself had an easy communication with his children, was aware of their impressions and little habits of mind.

"We like him," Demetri said. "But he is embarrassed, like Ava said."

"About what?"

I shrugged. "About nothing."

"You can't just be embarrassed about nothing," our father said.

"Really, about nothing."

"Nothing," Demi echoed. "Embarrassed at having to exist."

"Demetri!" Our father smiled. "Pretty good."

"Doctor"—our mother put her elbows on the table—"I'm sure Demetri seems very independent to you, but what I hope you can sense is that there is a fragility here. I hope you can see it."

"Marion," our father said, "I wouldn't say fragility."

"Well."

"I mean, I really wouldn't say fragility."

Udolph looked at our father and repeated, with only slight exhaustion, that she just thought it'd be good for him.

"I would love to know . . . thinking of it . . ." our mother began, "I would love to know why he excels in your French class. I do not speak French, and Demetri has never spoken of French. Not to me, at least." Here she turned to Demetri. I could tell her focus was on the zigzagged part in his hair, which she often ached to straighten. "Do you love French, Demi?"

Our father looked at him. He'd detached from the conversation, but he managed to smile: "Demetri! You're filled with *joie de vivre*?"

Demetri, not understanding, looked at me.

"Oh," I said. "They asked if you're just filled with a fart."

Our father snorted.

"Oh." Demetri paused. "Yes." He waited, let his face scrunch, and after a moment he lifted his leg and tooted a small one that was so round in sound and full of innocent frankness that I can hear it still. At the table we were silent until we erupted. Demetri smacked* me as he tried to catch his breath. I fell in a bundle off my chair. Our father watched us in his full smile. I heard our mother begin to stand.

From Demetri's new position he could see out the window above our sink. "The moon," he said. He stood up, showing the table his skirt. "Full, like I said . . ."

I sprang toward him and screamed at him not to look, recalling the blindness. He pulled me by the shirt and then held me in place. We were shrieking. "It won't," he said.

When I looked at the moon my eyes did go blank. After the blankness, there were deep tans, reds, yellow—and I seemed to occupy an entirely new position in space. The blindness, I knew, was showing me its first effects. I imagined an entire life in which all I saw were the shadows of a remembered world. For a moment I felt a sublime peace.

**Smacked*, oil on linen, small-medium
How many times I had to smack myself to try to re-create this sound as I stood there painting. This one is bright.

But in fact, the blankness was simply because our mother, keeping silent, had pulled me into the corner, where she'd pinched my eyelids with her nails and ripped a few lashes. In the next moment her voice was gentle in my ear.

"Please settle, honey," she said. She covered my eyes with her hands and kissed the top of my head. "I'm sorry. Please. Do not tell lies. And settle, settle."

I took a moment. My mother removed her hands and my sight returned to me in streaks of vision. I sat back down with Demetri's eyes hot on my left side. Soon I gathered the courage to look up at Dr. Udolph, who with her thin smile seemed to have registered nothing. In fact it was easy to imagine that she had been briefly lifted out of the room, and had just come back in, oblivious to all. I marveled at her stillness. Only later would I understand her response as a form of social intelligence, or cowardice.

After everyone was seated Dr. Udolph cleared her throat once more. Everything was lovely, lovely. She had had a lovely night, and it was so lovely to meet our family. She added—with a certain lightness now—that our mother should still consider the decision to send Demetri to the École, but she also understood, of course, if it was all too much, overwhelming, and that she should, regrettably, be leaving. She winked at Demetri and me on her way out.

A year ago I told Nati—our woman, that's how I think of her—I told her this whole Udolph story. She sat across from me at a quiet, sunken bar on Second Avenue and

Ninth Street. I told her how I think of the whole scene often, not necessarily because it involves Demetri, but because it was the last time our father seemed alive—it was before he went remote, room bound, with whatever remained of his will directed toward preserving his isolation, his weakness appalling to me. Or I wanted to tell her this. It'd have been lost on her. She was thinking only of Demetri, thinking he was going to die soon. She smiled as I spoke. I remember I looked hard at her mouth, her teeth (I am always drawn to teeth), hers long and pale gray at their upper ridges. Even now, writing and perched here on my stool, I imagine the toothbrush in her bathroom—a Dyson—the way it stands there skinny and servile. How she lets the battery die. How I bet it's dead right now.

At the bar she responded by staring at me. And by tapping her long clear nails on the table and saying something about her own family. Something about how she hated her father. I can hear her accented voice in my head, the way it turns sharp and ruthless even in its warmest cadence, how she goes on and on and on: "Do you know, when I was a child," is how she began, "when I was a child, back in Italy, I controlled everything. Everyone and everything. My father sat me down and said, 'Natalia, you are just like me. You are just like me.' I was disgusted at how badly he wanted us to be the same. I thought, no, we are not the same, because you do not know how to get what you want. I thought then—I will get exactly what I want. I will get everything I want so that I am not afraid to die. I will have everything already. By the time I die there'll be nothing left for me." She licked her lips to get the spritz off.

DEMETRI WAS STILL partly conscious as Nati and I sat there together in the sunken bar, nine or so months ago. He was conscious enough to desire death. Or death's aesthetics, its grotesque holiness.

After the drink with Nati I visited Demetri at his home. He was smiling. He was sitting up in his little makeshift hospital bed. A quilt lay over his legs. There were small red stains on the napkin draped across his chest, which is why I asked if he'd had cherries for lunch. When he said no, I asked if he had had a beet salad. No. Nothing with jam. No wine. "Well then I'm pretty sure there's a little blood on your little smock," I told him.

He looked down, veins gnarled his temples.

"I don't take it personally, Demetri," I said, moving toward him. "A little bloodletting. In fact, I'm sure it's a sign of honor, somewhere."

He sighed, removed the bloodied smock from its little clamps, crumpled it, and did not meet my eyes as he handed it to me. He smoothed the quilt over his chest. "How is it out there?" He asked, signaling to my coat. "Is the big experiment still going on?"

I began to unzip before I remembered that the room—

the only real room in his apartment, connected to the kitchen—was now repurposed and frigid with new air, a cold metallic tang that pressed the skin like cold spoons. "What experiment?" I asked.

Demetri raised his brows. His body's blue underhue, the skeletal lacework up his arms. I wanted to tell him how that morning I'd watched videos of his full-bodied self, my favorite performance of his, when he'd spoken on my behalf at an outdoor conference on "the new" in visual art, and then got drunk, stood on a table, and announced that a storm was careening through him. At the time of the video he'd just been fired and was trying to find something to break into, or out of.

"Is what still going on?" I asked again. I was standing over him. Mucus crust had lodged itself and was now crumbling out toward the ends of his eyes. He was sallow cheeked. He wasn't going to talk about anything real. I wondered if he smelled Nati on me. "The experiment where the sun comes up," he said, "and then the sun goes down. And the moon comes up, goes down." His eyes flashed. "And then the sun again. And everyone kind of ambles around."

"Oh," I said, "that big one." He wanted me to carry it on—to play. No refusing him. "Yes, the experiment is still going on."

He nodded, considered. Brows still high. "What stage is it in?"

I settled into the armchair placed at the foot of his bed. "It's in peer review."

Demetri collapsed his brows, like this was grave but expected news. "Being reviewed. By who?" He paused. I knew—from the lilt in his silence—that he wanted to answer his own question, so I waited. The waiting used to frustrate me. Pauses were for shy children, I thought, or the geriatric. Now I let them run their course. "Everything's reviewed by the Celestial Council," he said.

I'd lost our train of thought. "By the Celestial Council," I repeated him, held his smock tight in my fist.

"Will they like me?"

"They'll know better."

"Such cowards." He considered. "I want more of a terrestrial council."

"Judge Judy."

"Yes," he said. Just then the nurse came in. "She'd adore me."

I liked this nurse for her indifference toward me. She walked straight toward Demetri's bed, then turned around, twisted her hips in his direction. I stayed silent as Demetri observed her, picked up her details—daddy longleg lashes, candy-blue cotton stretched tight around her thighs.

At last she turned to face him. "Demetri, where is your smock?"

Demetri pointed at me. "She stole it," he said. I wondered if I should tell her I still had it, was holding it in my hand. But she moved speedily along—an efficient smile as she reached across Demi's chest to adjust a tray. "So," Demetri asked the nurse as she loomed over him, "do I look like I'm melting?"

"No," she answered, realigning a cable and returning to his side. "Why, you're hot? You feel hot?" Her fuchsia nails glinted as she lowered his quilt from his chest to his hips. She turned and bent down to pull out a new stack of smocks.

"Don't say it, Demetri." I pretended to cower. When it came to women, illness had reduced him to cliché. It gave him phrases he'd never have touched. *Not as hot as you look*. I could feel it coming.

But Demetri was somewhere else. "No . . . just a little itchy," he said. "Feels a little wet." His voice sounded clogged. I looked again at what I'd taken—in a brief reprieve from reality—for a shadow beneath his nose. It was blood, bright, falling soft from his nose into his mouth.

He began to smack his lips.

I stood up and went to him.

I pulled his smock from my pocket and used it to wipe his nose and mouth. It couldn't absorb much. I tried to tilt his head back as I dabbed. Demetri was calm. He closed his eyes and smiled, his lips stained red. "Better. And how honored are you now, Ava?" he asked me. "A mark of a high priest to revive the dead."

But he was still bleeding. When he next opened his

mouth a thin red membrane spread between his lips. I watched it form into a bubble. At his next breath it burst, spraying tiny blood pellets* on his chin. "Ava."

The nurse moved me aside, used a moist wipe to clean him; she tilted his head forward instead of backward and placed a clamp at the bridge of his nose. I stepped away to better watch their movements. "Thanks," he kept trying to say as she cleaned him. "Thanks. Thank you." (It was his special brand of thank-you: we're out, we're dressed up, we're late for something, someone holds a door for us and Demetri jogs with lazy athleticism to catch it, breathing, *Thanks, thank you*—he reaches the door, looks back at me—*Move, Ava.*) The nurse stabilized him. He whispered nonsense, thanked her again, kept his eyes closed.

The smock was wet with new blood when I placed it back in my pocket.

"Ava." The nurse pulled me toward the kitchen. Artwork by Demetri's friends hung along the opposite wall. Posters from movies he'd helped to produce: an ancient army of men, a sepia pair of Dust Bowl boys, a Victorian woman standing in the woods, emitting lots of strong obscure emotions. There was a rough sketch of Demetri himself, drawn by Nati. And then there was a massive sketch

---

****Pellets***, watercolor and blood on rice paper, small-medium
Hard to get the exact intensity of blood with a medium like watercolor. I completed this on the same day as *Crystallizing*, so got a little bit of real thumb blood in there.

by me, a slice of bread bursting into flames, hung like a hearth at the end of the row.

"He is going to vomit," the nurse whispered to me. "It's the third bleeding since the morning. Not bad. But he's been swallowing." She said something else. Blood as a digestive irritant. Other things. I focused on the French braid traveling tight along the right side of her head. So tight. Militant. Did that hair turn her into a nurse? Or did nursehood lead her to the hair? She kept talking. An unequipped stomach. Medically induced regurgitation. "You have to leave."

I nodded and wandered back into the room. "Demetri." He was lying still, his eyes closed, the clamp like a butterfly stuck on his nose. "I'm going home for a bit," I said. "I have to change into my white linens. A robe, too, I think."

"Okay," he said. I didn't think he got it.

"I'll be back, with miracles," I added, arching forward.

I waited. He was silent. I pressed into the strain. Nothing. I wanted to say please. I realized, then, that he was giving me a thumbs-up from under his quilt. "Priest," he said. "Go tend."

WHEN I LEFT HIM I walked five blocks north, to the memorial park on Seventh Avenue and Greenwich. In the city certain parks have a shrapnel aspect. They are violent fragments of greenery, wedged hard into the in-betweens. This one, across from the now demolished St. Vincent's hospital, is cut by the surrounding avenues into a long, narrow triangle. I chose a bench on the hypotenuse. I looked at the purple moor and forest grass expressing fever dreams of the city's former verdant lush. I looked at the benches around me. I looked at the dogs.

After seeing Demetri I'd try to blot the whole thing out: everything he said, what he looked like on that bed, the sound of his breath, I'd obliterate it. If there was a healthy body next to me, I'd try to shovel Demetri into it. I'd try to think of other things. Animals. What kind of wood they used for the bench I was sitting on. Who painted it. Who supplied the paint. If I'd ever bought paints of the same family. I'd think of men. Of sitting on the bench with men. I'd think of attraction. Anything. That day, after our visit, I sat there thinking of the last time I had—or, as it was, did not have—sex with a man: Daniel. I'd seen him around at Bar Down. Severe, lean wrists. I'd watch his veins twitch when he signed his bill. Then one night he was alone. "Well, how about you come up," I said to him. I'd just had forty-eight hours of painting and no yield. Something in me needed to break, then become.

I brought him to my bed, laid him down, mounted, he moaned, his head reared into the pillow with his neck grown cocktaut.

Then my phone rang. Demetri. I didn't answer. It rang

again. When I picked up he was breathless: "Ava, you have to come. I broke my clavicle."

I try to whisper: "Can you get it replaced?"

"What?"

"What's a clavicle?"

"My collarbone."

"But you have two?"

"Ava."

An hour later we met at the hospital. He was fine. They gave him pain relievers and put his arm in a nylon sling. We took the train home. Demetri moaned when another man pressed into him. The two women standing beside him looked at him with urgent maternal attention.

I'd seen that look before. The mothers of our childhood friends. Teachers. Our elementary school nurse—he would go to her with concerns of varying degrees: he thought he was balding, that a flesh-eating bacteria had embedded itself in an open wound, that his retina was in the process of detaching. At one point he was convinced blood was dripping down his back. For this one, they called me in. I walked into her office to find Demetri shirtless, panicked.* "Look." He kept taking my hand, placing it on his back, and making me feel the blood—which was only bare skin

*_**Panicked**_, oil on linen, large
This image will look like one huge spine to you.

moistened from the sweat gathered in his panic. I had him face me. His eyes were hollow by then. They'd been pressed deeper into his skull and the color had drained to a milk blue. He calmed down. The nurse had him put his shirt back on. Demetri left the room in peace, but he turned to me on his way out, suspicious.

I stayed in the room with the nurse. I'd seen the way she touched him. I took my own shirt off and asked if she might touch me, too. She smiled, had me lie down, ran her hands down my spine, some kind of path toward him.

Talk about beauty. The beginnings. Sometimes Demetri and I are asked if we grew up on art in a specific instructional sense. They ask if we were trained, if I was shown how to paint and if Demetri was shown how to look at things. We were not. The beauty magazines our mother devoured are the kind you know: stiff and lacquered, stuffed with women hanging in limp geometric shapes. Our father did know how to stop and stare at a tree, or a field of trees. But he did this too often, where it became less about the trees and more about the expanse of his silence.

But our father was the one who took us to the museum. We went three times, always the Met. He would get us through the door and then would either sit in the café, or stand and stare at a massive marble bust of Caesar, or touch the items in the gift shop, all as Demetri and I roamed around.

We knew ourselves to be in a place with a tempting number of breakable items. We prided ourselves on this. We felt a savage possession over the severed heads of antiquity, the medieval jewels—fat drops of jade, turquoise set in gold, all our bounty.

We entered the European sculpture wing, at the southern end, and I lost it. Hard to breathe. The room was too large. This was the first time I realized so much empty space above your head can compress you, stunt your chest and breath. The walls were made entirely of glass. Huge swaths of sun broke open the floor, spread slantwise over clusters of marble bodies.

"How many of us could fit in here?" I asked Demetri on our first visit. He closed his eyes and tried to do the mental calculation. "It depends on how we're stacked."

In the near center of the room was my first artistic challenge: a massive sculpture, a balletic bundle of agony, composed of four naked, starving boys surrounding their naked, starving father, who looked too much like our own father, sitting there with his fingers peeling his lips apart. I stared at the family. Limbs and muscles, bubbling out through stone. I wondered how something so solid could be so throbbing.

I did not get near enough to read the label, and so I did not know who the boys were, or why they were starving, until on our third visit Demetri rushed over to me. I could tell he'd learned something new by the way he walked, all glossed up. The father is named Ugolino, Demi told me, and he and his sons are in the depths of hell.

"Why are they down there?"

On our previous two visits Demetri had tottered around as I sketched. He'd looked more at the labels than the pieces themselves. He'd mumbled to himself the names and dates that I failed to keep in memory. That day he had left me to go upstairs and came back to tell me he saw paintings that looked like they were plugged into the wall because of the colors' neon brightness; he told me there were painted balls of glass rolling off painted tables. It was the last time he spoke of art this way. "Nipples." He squeezed his own. "The kind of fat that looks like cheese." Then he turned to Ugolino and his starving children. "They're down there because the mother wanted her Alone Time." We considered this likely. It was the kind of time our mother requested. "Really, Ava, but I shouldn't tell you, it's that the boys want their father to eat them. Not to save them. To eat them."

I looked again at the starving boys, feeling they'd betrayed me. It had always seemed to me that they wanted to be saved. "I can't tell."

"They want to die. I heard it from her." Demi pointed to a tour guide, who was just then whispering at people, waving her arms all around.

"You know," I said, "that's you." I pointed toward Ugolino, and then directly at the smallest starving boy. His belly was tucked and tight in that way of active, small boys; his head wilted, limping back into his shoulders.

"It's not me!" Demetri grabbed the air in anger. "I'm not that small. And I don't go like *this*." He organized his body like the boy's, then snapped back to normal. "Have you ever seen me go like *this*?" He again went limp like the boy.

But then he agreed to be drawn. Together we angled his body to mirror the boy's.

Seeing me with a pencil and paper, some visitors stopped to watch. Their gaze tempted Demetri into action. I saw him begin to say hello. I knew he must have memorized much of what the guide said earlier and had been waiting to express it all to someone with more patience.

"Stay still," I told him.

I started with his legs, which were bare and easily recreated. His calves came out bold and right, the one angled behind the other. But as I worked my way up his body I realized there were faint shadows across the abdomen I'd need to get right. "You need to take that off," I told him, pointing at his shirt. Demetri said no. He was wearing a white turtleneck, a short-sleeved item our mother bought him because she thought it looked French. When he undressed it'd catch at the edge of his nose, forcing him and my mother to tug it hard around his skull.

I walked to where he was standing. We started slow, peeling from the hemline and up over his head. But when the shirt wouldn't budge Demetri cracked. He pulled the spandex tight over the top half of his face and suddenly became larval. The shirt stretched into a white film over his nose and eyes. I could feel his frustration mounting. Energy climbed with heat to the crown of his head. Demetri heaved twice before he broke. He tore through the gallery. He kept the shirt over his nose and eyes as he ran.* He began feigning asphyxiation. He darted around the corner, out of the room, into Perseus. He came back again. Everyone watched him. No one moved.

When the guard yelled at us it was not because of Demetri, but because I, too, had started shrieking, chasing him not to help him but to see him better. As he ran he screamed at nobody. He pointed at me. My eyes began to water. We both could barely see.

Soon we were captured, forced into a corner, made to sit down. Demetri explained to the guard that he was diseased. I watched him think about with what. The guard told us we could go back to our sketching after twenty minutes of complete silence.

We agreed. The time passed. We waited for the guard's nod, and then were up again. I stood Demetri before the sculpture. Again I posed him. Demetri whispered to me as I drew.

"You know what disease I said?" he asked. "Methemoglobinemia." He pronounced every syllable. "Do you know

---

**Ran*, oil on paper, large
I'm realizing this painting is much more an image of an ecstatic echo.

what that is?" I went on drawing, focused at last, until I felt him pointing. I followed his finger to the youngest boy, lying prone on his father's leg. "This son is dead."

"How do you know?"

"The guide," he said.

"You can be him if you want."

"I'm not dead," he said. He swerved his body to talk to the boy. "You are," he said. "Is it okay?"

"Demetri," I said.

He groaned at high pitch.

"Stop."

The groan grew. We saw the guard begin to approach. No one wanted a scene. As Demetri released his scream—high, liquid—he turned on his heel and ran. The sound made me stand still. Demetri did not turn to make sure I was following. My knees kicked in and I sprinted.

I DON'T KNOW where that recklessness goes in a person. I can see now how often as an adult I'd try to get it out of him—I'd try to find it like a lost person traveling inside him. Twice last fall I lay down flat outside his apartment building, out on the sidewalk, wearing a red leotard and holding a massive bow and arrow that I bought at a child's Halloween store. I wanted to watch him turn the corner, see me, and react. The first time he only helped me up in silence and then walked calmly in the opposite direction.

The second time we went for coffee. Often, he'd enter my apartment with his eyes closed because he knew I'd be naked, walking around. He'd stand there in my open doorway with his eyes closed talking to me about his day, asking me questions, refusing any outrage, letting me wave hello to my neighbors. He refused to match me on the terms I wanted, outmatching me on his own.

The refusal was long-standing. I can place it to the day I was broken open by a chubby boy named Vincent and told Demetri about it. I was sixteen. We were sitting at Han Dynasty, three blocks from our Long Island home. "Virginity is under-understood," I was telling him. We were sitting there in our metal ribbed-back chairs, leaning over the linoleum table, picking food off our metal trays. I knew that day exactly what Demetri planned to say to me and had to discuss my change first. "The *pain* . . ." I was saying to him. "The pain felt somehow like my fault, not like his. He came just trying to get inside me and that was a mess. Then he fucked me like I was dead. And when he finished he shouted something, I think it was 'FIVE.'" Demetri flinched as I spoke. "I looked at the color, the pink glaze he'd spilled, and I thought: that's gentle. But I realized it was because a little blood was laced through it, just a very little. Virgins should never fuck virgins. No one told me."

"Ava." Demetri looked around, nervous. "You are screaming."

"Demetri, I am telling you an amazing story."

"I'm sorry." His whole head seemed to shut down. He hooked his fingers in his mouth. Removed them. Hooked them back in his mouth. Removed them. A tic from boyhood. He sighed. His curls soft over his forehead. "I got the letter today."

"From?" But I knew. I'd seen it—large, acceptance size.

"Harvard." Demetri watched me carefully. He said it like he didn't mean to be so proud of himself. His next sip of water was to tell me he'd gotten in.

I coughed and then sat up, waited too long. I had prepared for this. Still, nothing. I reached out and put my palm on the table between us, spread my fingers out wide—an offering.

"Thank you. I have two already," he said, showing me his hands. "But it's a nice gesture."

I told him it was fantastic.

He nodded—"Yeah"—and turned his attention outside, across the street. The sky crammed its gray into his eyes so that he looked sick, overcharged.* It grew clear to me that there was something else in him—new in him—that I did not know. I wanted to ask, but by then I'd made a rule of ignoring Demi's outside gazes. They were too self-obsessed. I looked away and considered how best to disrupt him with one of my three recent successes, like my newly finished

---

**Overcharged*, acrylic on canvas board, large
Overcharged eyes. I mixed a kind of computer-blue with black and gray, the density concentrated just left of center.

painting, or the supposedly exciting new shape of my cunt, or my newly acquired client (who was thirteen, paying me in Trident and bagels for a surreptitious portrait of her love, whose picture was warping in my pocket).

I looked up, having settled on the first of these. But by the time I started to speak, Demi's whole face had shifted again. He'd grown flush—prophetic—with a quiet exhilaration. I realized he was proud of himself for reasons that had nothing to do with me. "And, you know," I said quickly, "you're really not cut out to *make* history, Demetri." I shrugged. "It really takes a certain kind of mentality, and you don't have it." I took a forkful of rice. "There are makers of history, there are teachers of history, and learners of history. It's good you know which you are. I mean that you don't like making things. Like history. Instead you love categories and categorizing. All that kind of thing."

I looked down and felt him nod. "Okay," he said.

Demetri, I told myself, sitting across from him, would never have to ask a question again. His life would play out in a constant stream of answers. Demetri would be so smart that he'd never even have to think. For him, the timeline of the world would extend ever deeper into the past as his conception of the future broadened, until his knowledge took him over and he'd forget to think anything real at all.

Across the table Demetri was speaking again, using his hands in ways I didn't understand, though I could tell by his tone that he'd forgiven me for what I'd said, and this forgiveness disturbed me. When rice tickled the back of my throat I gagged and reached for my napkin. Demetri thought it was a joke.

"You're being a child," he said. But then in one slow, extended move he took a long sip of water. He jutted out his bottom row of teeth, bent a bit forward, and let his jaw go slack. Water streamed down his chin, into his turtleneck. His eyes glazed* over.

I sat up. "Demetri . . ." I said. But he only opened his mouth farther, let more water come down. I yelled at him to stop. He didn't budge, so I laughed. When I threw my head back, he finally sat up.

"That's been you," he said, wiping his chin. "This whole time."

"It hasn't."

"Ava. Do you just zone out when we're not talking about you?"

"I honestly wouldn't know."

He adjusted himself. I knew then that if he was not going to continue to integrate our interests this would be my job. And so when he fell in love for the first time I was on it. The girl was Willow. She was a German Mexican with

---

**Glazed*, oil and egg wash on linen, medium
Egg wash on there because I thought it might give me the glaze I needed. When Demetri's eyes glaze over they look like vats of blue lard. Anyway, the egg hasn't worked yet. We'll see.

the looks of an all-American. She'd sprung out of someone's perfectly trimmed, sun-warmed front lawn. She was very nice and smiled often. She stood tan and tall. She held convictions about what was stupid, what was smart, what was wrong, what was right (yellow shoes, her friend Alan, animal abuse, having good parents).

Demetri woke before school one morning, splotched and hot, and told me that for the seventh night in a row he'd dreamed of her. "The dreams are long and delirious," he said. "And if I see her today I'm going to throw up."

The dreams continued. Sometimes he and Willow had a picnic and pressed their palms together. Sometimes he was sitting on her lap on the toilet and felt the vibration of her pee hitting the water. Sometimes she was strangling him, biting his tongue, until she bit it all the way off, and they continued. Under no circumstances did Demetri speak to her—not in his dreams, and not in real life.

We'd pass her in the hallway. She'd be chatting with a friend, and I'd urge Demetri to say something so that maybe together we could pursue it. Sometimes I'd hear him revving up. He'd start to form a word. But she would pass us quickly. Demetri would walk after her but would lose his rhythm, trip, everything thrown. Most often he managed to stay still and breathe hard. Or sometimes just: "Jesus."

To help him get out of the house in the mornings we blasted music as we packed our things. "Do you think he can hear us?" Demetri would ask of our father. But by then our father used earbuds. He'd sit in his room, trying to work, helping to edit commercial scripts, trying to figure out ways to invest his small inheritance. He did not take well to sun but still he'd go out to do our grocery shopping, made sure our freezer was stocked with frozen fruit and Hungry-Mans. He never made a decision for us. He never yelled. He'd emerge from his room on our birthdays. He'd come out with the video camera and would place it on the counter and film the three of us as we sang, would interview us on our goals for the year, as if his helping us to inaugurate our growth would incorporate him into it. Sometimes—maybe two or three nights in the year—Demetri would put cherries and sliced cheese on a platter, and he and my father would sit on the couch and watch a movie. Usually some important film made by a man whose artful Italian name kept me away. From the other room I'd hear him say, "Demetri, this tracking shot . . ." or "This kind of patience in a scene has evaporated . . ." He'd lift his arm to point at the screen with languor and fervor, like God reaching toward Adam, only if Adam were a screen and God could not get his finger straight. For Demetri these statements from our father were something like the last bits of meaning anyone would ever express. I was forced to pass the two of them on my way to my room. Usually I looked away, but if I ever looked in their direction, only Demetri looked up and offered me a dumb, half-apologetic smile.

But back to our mornings: "Will you try today?" I'd ask him of Willow.

He wouldn't. He'd come home sullen. Day after day of this, I began waiting for him to give it up. Everything that he was good at had to come naturally. Willow was not coming at all.

Until, that is, a month after the first dream. I watched it happen. Her locker was near ours, and as she made room for Demetri to pass behind her, she turned and said: "Sorry about that!"

Demetri stopped us. He cleared his throat. "Where is your sweater from?" he asked her. I thought this was too femme a question and waited for her cruelty.

Instead, she stepped back and observed her chest with incredible seriousness. "This?" Her top was cable-knit, with an obscure animal embroidered near her neck. "I made this myself."

I looked at Demetri and watched him swallow. "Wow," he said.

She smiled. "Thanks!"

The school day had just ended. In the exodus to the lot I stayed a couple paces behind as I watched them walk together. There was no speech between them, or none that I could hear. Still, the meaner, sharper part of me—the part that likes to splinter off and rule the rest of me from a distance—that part was sure that Willow was showing my brother some irremediable assortment of deficiencies. But I thought this only halfway. Because in truth the vision of them overwhelmed me. I watched them walk—something eternal about their bodies side by side. They moved as if cast together out of the same ancient realm.

Demetri had had crushes before. But with each of those girls I'd managed to tag along. If something stood out about a girl's mole, I thought I could see it, too. If Demetri saw a good pair of ears, a scar that endeared him, or gaps in teeth (those would come later, with Nati), I saw the same. We'd discuss faces on the way to school, or standing in the kitchen, or in the backseat of someone's mother's SUV. "That's true," I'd say. And we'd both begin our fascination. It never occurred to me, when I was younger, that Demetri would be attracted to someone without me. Because different desires would make us what we were not—namely, two separate people.

Later on the same day they walked together, Demetri and I stood by the stove in our kitchen, lighting bread on fire in the open flame, and Demetri told me what he had seen Willow do and say. She ate Starbursts, and he watched as she used a chipped nail to unpeel only the pink squares, kept watching as she rolled the wrappers into a ring and then put the ring around her thumb, put her thumb against her nose.

"Is it strange," he asked me, standing against the refrigerator sprinkling salt over a skewer of creminis, "that every time she laughs I want to die. Or that every time she bends forward on her chair . . ." He slid the skewer down his throat, pulled off the mushrooms with his teeth, talked as he chewed. "In gym," he said, "she puts her hair over the front of her face. Except her nose always sticks out between the strands because it has that sharp slope. And then she tilts her head back and the hair parts, divided by her nose, like a curtain for her smile."

"That's too poetic."

"I know. I wrote it down."

"You should write it to her."

"I feel like I have to look at her first, I mean at the same time that she looks at me. We need more contact." He insisted he was taking his time. Something between them was growing. "It's going to happen."

I only grew more impatient. Demetri, I thought, was putting us through all of this and had not even the strength to start a private conversation. He couldn't give her a note.

I'd have encouraged him even harder, but by then I had seen an image—once I'd seen it, I could not stop seeing it. Demetri had been reading, studying for a competition to do with the history of religion in France, and the book had a painting on its cover. It was a picnic scene. Up close in the foreground: a naked woman, breasts out. Two men sat beside her—both talking to her, both fully attired in pants and layered jackets—but it was she in her nakedness who stared at me.

Luncheon on the Grass, Demetri told me when I asked. The cover listed no painter. I studied it hard. I'd seen women naked before—my mother's body, and my own, and endless others in movies, in locker rooms. But this woman's nakedness was strong. Her skin was a thick fabric—she wore five layers of naked for every cloth layer on the men. Even more than her body, her face: I loved the way she looked at me. I slid down the black borders of her eye, her orbital socket, which fused down into her nose. Her breasts these unnippled orbs. And then—lower—the folds in her belly, her girthy thighs—stark strength and solidity. One dirty heel.

I wanted to mock or even to question my attachment to her, but I could not. This woman was never going to pretend to laugh at a joke. She'd never seek dangerous pleasures just for the thrill of renouncing them. She was real down to the base of every desire. You could tell from her gaze that she was superior, outside the orbit of her body, indifferent about it. She was present with the men, only looking at me quick to say, *Sorry, but we three are talking.*

It took me a number of views to realize that through some spiritual undercurrent, through some parallel in the clean indifference, what I kept finding in her was Willow.

At school, I stood at my locker and waited for her. When she came by I told her that for my next project I would need a female model. She didn't hesitate. I brought out Demetri's book and showed her the painting on the cover. I made sure to say the word "nude" instead of "naked." Willow studied the painting. I watched her blink twice. She wasn't just pretending to think, and at last she stood back and nodded: "Sure, I've modeled nude before." She said it without pretension. She smiled at the painting, and then when she shifted her eyes from the book toward my face I tried to fall in love with her—peach lips, breath cool and thin. It didn't happen. I nodded. A part of me suspected she'd say yes. I knew this even though Demetri, who hated being drawn, was always surprised when people agreed to sit for me. I often felt pride that I understood something he didn't, which was that people want to be depicted not because they want to be captured as they really are, or as more than they really are, but because they want to be shown what others think they really are, which is most important to them.

The next day, after school, Willow met me in the art room. The windows faced the courtyard, so the light in the room was dark and verdant. I led Willow into a large closet at the back end that I used as my studio. I gave her the blue towel I'd brought for her to sit on, provided her a copy of the *Luncheon*, and told her how to pose. As she undressed, I kept my eyes down and configured the lights.

"Okay," I heard her say.

Willow's body. A part of me is shy about mentioning it because I still think Demetri will wake up and read this. I'll be brief and will only say that her body surprised me.

Willow—I wanted to tell her—there is something eminently geometric about you, like you want me to lift you and place you in a box, so you can mock its geometry with the perfection of your own. (Lately I'd been trying to feel more intelligent.) I lifted my brush and started at her collarbone. From there I worked my way down ridges of upper rib and didn't lift my brush until I reached the middle of her breast, which ended at a nippled point—an embossed square, so precise—on which her whole body might rock if you were to suddenly push her over.

She stared at me as she posed. She didn't even move when, realigning her hair, I very lightly brushed my lips against hers. It was so small. She stayed so still. I wondered if she'd even felt it. She continued to stare at me, and I'll admit I again began to feel a surge of something, a weightlessness, because I thought her eyes—wide, pale brown—I thought her eyes might be exposing a depth of feeling. She continued in her silence, which also made me curious. Didn't she want to tell me how interesting this was? Or that she was pleased to do it? Didn't she wonder if maybe she should've washed her hands to wipe off the marker on her wrist? Did she wonder where I'd be looking the hardest? Where and when to suck in? Nothing seemed to bother her. I thought maybe I'd found her distilled self. I convinced myself that a certain wisdom seeped from her like breath. It frightened me. I wanted to say, Keep it to yourself. But she was in my hands, and suddenly seized with the seriousness of what I was doing, I began to laugh. Willow still did not budge.

I finished the painting, excited to show Demetri, and kept my head down as Willow put her clothes back on in a series of yanks and smoothings over. She told me she wished to see what I'd done but did not mind when I told her I'd show her the next day, after I let it dry overnight and completed the finishing touches. She nodded. She moved as if we were in a solemn mutual understanding, and I envied the version of myself with whom she had this special relationship.

I took the canvas home. Demetri would see that I'd had the courage to do what he couldn't—I saw the girl naked, I got her to stare at me, I did not flinch from her gaze, I knew her all the way around. It might be true that I uncovered a depth in her. I was on the other side of something. I knew more than he did. I was not just a part of his desire, but ahead of it. It would be his job to meet me. He would take a certain pride in this and would be aware of the subtlety in my accomplishment. He would be grateful. We would both be in.

THAT NIGHT Demetri happened to be ecstatic. He was standing by the sink, telling me that between lunch and gym he met Willow by the lockers, just as she was resetting her lock. When she smiled at him he had to look away. He was getting somewhere. "Because she didn't want to talk," he said. "But in an inviting kind of way."

I walked toward the den, toward my canvas, which I had placed—along with my other work—against the wall to dry. Lifting it over my head, I brought it toward Demetri and flipped it around.

The background—which was only a bit of creased blue towel—was still merely sketched, only partway filled with paint, so when Demetri stood still, looking at the work, and then when his neck twitched, and then when he did not speak, I thought he was annoyed at my having left things unfinished.

"I'm not sure—" he began. He looked closer. I watched his eyes, the way he worked his way down her body. He was silent. His ears lit up in their upper corners—a hollow* red.

"Your ears, Demi," I said, cupping my own.

"Where did you get this?"

I told him I painted it.

He wasn't looking at me. "How?" He began to breathe heavily.

"With a brush." I didn't mention how close I'd brought my face to her face.

**Hollow*, acrylic and smoke and soot on canvas, medium
Can't tell you how disgusting my apartment smelled after I tried to light this red acrylic paint on fire. Kind of satisfying.

Still, he didn't speak. "Did you tell her it was for me?" Then he looked at me. I felt a steep break in my stomach.

"I didn't say it was for you . . . I said it was for nothing. Or that maybe it was for us."

"What does that mean?"

We waited.

Demetri didn't look at me as he lifted the canvas and placed it face down on the counter. He walked toward the wooden knife block. I thought of the butcher knife running through Willow's painted body. Her skull bursting open, water spilling from her gut. I realized I was hoping he would puncture her so we could both see that beneath her body was only the blue air of our own home. (I wanted, I realize now, for our father to come in and see what I had done, and for him to be amazed at my skill, and for him to convince Demetri of it.)

Demetri was not reaching for a knife. He had only left his book near the block. The book was large with small print at the bottom that said "a novel." It was nothing I'd ever read. He picked it up and walked toward the back door. I stayed still. He opened the door, continued walking out, and was triplicated, refracted into three by the glass frame. At high speed, my mind repeated the image—his three somber heads, declining* in posture—until the glass rattled shut. When I blinked Demetri was out on the patio.

**Declining*, oil on trifold wooden panel, small

I walked to the window. Demetri wiped ants off the lawn chair and lay down. His face was to the yard. I waited in the kitchen for an hour. Then another half. Then I moved to the den, where I could see him better. Still, all I saw were his legs, crossed at the ankles, his hands holding his book. Just an eighth of his face in profile. We didn't go into the yard often, because the trees we planted would not grow, and all we could see was the Sound. He knew I would not follow. I stood and watched him. I waited for him to flip a page of his book. When he didn't I wondered if he had fallen asleep. Everything about him was static. I soothed myself into thinking he'd forgotten everything—or remembered everything about something else. Except that I noted, tilting far forward, his ear burned still.

DEMETRI WOULD PAUSE ME here and suggest I refocus, that I go back to Willow, explain that Demetri did not speak to me for a week or so, but that anyway, Willow fizzled as an object of desire, that Demetri continued to mistake her incuriosity for some kind of deep stoicism, until he realized her affect was not a mistake and concluded

---

Declining (cont.): It was very hard to find a small Renaissance-style trifold wooden panel (but I was uncompromising—I needed this one piece to be more literal in its depiction of Demetri's three heads as he walked out that back door), so I made the trifold myself, and as I was hammering in the hinges my neighbor knocked on the door to ask if I was hungry, because he had some leftover cake from his birthday party. It was a good cake.

she really was too mature for him; he might also suggest I take time to write of his other pursuits and successes—the prizes, the adoration—so that he doesn't look incapable, but I can't stop now.

I am writing this, I realize, portrait by portrait, as my eyes move along my wall, studying what I have made of him.

He's in his dorm room. He's reading. I've come with him to Harvard. I didn't ask. He didn't say no. I just went, having no idea the cultural cachet that not earning my GED would later afford me, no idea it'd be very chic to be formally undereducated. On the floor of his dorm room, under the wire frame of his bed, I set up my own makeshift living space: not a mattress but a thick enough mattress pad, blue sheets from the hardware store, a quilt. I'd lie down and sketch my view obsessively—Demetri's wire mattress frame, the actual mattress puffing out between the wire squares, a foot or so above my face. I'd push my finger up into the bubbled fabric.

"*Stop*," Demetri would say from above me.

"You can feel that?" I could always tell where he was on the bed based on which squares were puffing and which were taut.

At the time, I was drawing everything. I took a visual inventory of every item in his room. Every pen, Post-it, notebook, gnarled staple, binder clip. The withered spine of every book. The crumpled bits of paper that looked like ancient white pebbles. Then I'd leave his room and make detailed sketches of the shower drains, the hair woven through the various spokes. I turned these into my first formal three-by-three-inch grid series. I drew the yellowed, curdled paint bubbling off the bathroom stall in grotesque efflorescence. I drew basic landscapes, the slow slopes of walkways. I drew Harvard boys walking in army greens and khakis. Boys in button-downs and slacks. The gym boys in winter with spandex tights under their athletic shorts. I drew the red bricks of buildings at dusk, when the light turned the hard stone into powder. I drew the underbelly of green leaves. I drew the campus church and tried to capture the translucence of the stained glass. On the day I ran out of paper I took down his curtains and painted on those. And I drew myself, too many times, always avoiding my face.

One day I entered Demetri's room and all of my sketches were gone. Nothing on his desk, nothing in my bin, nothing in my folders under the bed. Without checking to see if anything else was missing, I began to panic. My shoulders felt flooded with blood and I could not speak. An ache began to pulse deep in my stomach. I figured Demetri was in class and I was about to do something strange—call my father—when at once Demetri came in. He was breathless. "They're deinstalling," he said. His arms were overloaded with paper. All my work, I recognized it at once. "Wait. Sorry." He caught his breath. "They're deinstalling the work at Corner soon and need someone new, and in a rush I brought yours over, to see if maybe they'd hang some stuff."

His favorite café, Corner, hung work by local artists for a couple months at a time—they marked each piece with a price. Sometimes they sold.

"Did they want any of it?"

"No," Demi said, spilling all my rejection on the bed. "But maybe if you have a relevant theme . . . like coffee, they'd take it."

I told him that'd be gauche, neo-Warhol-kitsch. Still, for the next three days, as Demetri went to class, I walked around campus and posed my Styrofoam to-go cups in various prominent positions. I went into students' communal kitchens and gathered all the mugs I could find—clay and glazed, steely with an enamel finish, plain porcelain chipped along the rim. I drew them upside down with coffee spilling out, the squat ones as if they were affable little bodies. I tried to turn my hand deep into the curves. Demetri took the sketches over to Corner, and Corner agreed to hang them. I was proud, though in their three months of hanging I did not visit them. They were not my idea, I felt. They were conceptually small and had nothing to do with me. I didn't want to read my name next to them. In the end only one of eleven sold—the rest were returned to us.

It didn't matter. By the end of the semester, I was drawing so often that I got myself into the local paper. Zara, a young woman living in Demetri's building, would sit next to me in the lobby of the disease dynamics research center (it had the best light) and watch me sketch in colored pencil. At first she was silent. She'd watch my paper as I drew a boy sitting by a window. She watched me fail to foreshorten his legs. Or she'd watch me draw a group of plaid-laden girls eating lunch at the table near the exit. She laughed—one of her first audible sounds—when I had trouble sketching the boundaries between the girls' chopsticks and fingers. The wood bled into knuckles. I asked if she could do it better. She took my pad and showed me that yes, she could.

Back then I often felt myself—I still feel myself—miniaturize people to better pin and wield them into objects of creation. Zara was no exception to this. I asked her if she could move away from me so I could sketch her, and without speaking she moved to sit in the chair I pointed to and stayed so still I forgot she was a living being, even as I sketched her parted mouth, which quivered at the intake of air. She was short and round with a small face. She had precisely two chins, which pulled into one when she lifted her head to check for a spider on the ceiling. The first time I gave her a sketch she did not look at me, she only nodded and smiled and sat back down beside me.

Once I brought her an unfinished sketch of Demetri. "Yes, I know this boy," she whispered. "He's supposed to be smart." She took the sketch and studied it in silence, and then handed it back. "You do others better," she said. I told her Demetri was my brother. "So you'll never see him, really. Though I think you were starting to get the nose."

Zara began to intern at the *Gazette*. They gave her a camera to aid in her reporting. She took photos of me and my work as I drew, although she only captured me when I was adjusting, erasing, or completely reconfiguring. "Do you ever finish anything?" she asked me. I brought her my first finished sketchbook, completed at age fifteen. The book was full—mostly with nudes of myself, always starting at the neck. It was clear I had been trying to perfect the basics: the simple weight of bone inside skin, the torque of abdomen, padded skin over the navel. Demetri was in there, too, clothed, unaware of my attention. Zara had me hold the sketches to the light as she took photos of her favorites.

A month or so later she came to me with her newspaper in hand. She opened to the Arts section and I saw them: four photos of my work—two nudes of my faceless self and two portraits of Demetri. The article was titled, simply, "Local Artists," and the text itself didn't mention me by name—only the caption. "They just needed pictures," Zara said, tilting her chin toward me. "Are you going to celebrate?"

I told her yes and called Demetri. As the phone rang I imagined us driving, both looking up and seeing my face spread across a massive sheet of vinyl overlooking a five-lane interstate.

"You are where?" he asked when he picked up.

"In the paper. I am *inside* of the paper. So are you." He said to come right away. He was at a new, small café working before his date with his most recent girl, Rose. "It won't be a long date," he told me. "But I'm very excited for it." He'd been working hard in the film studies program, harassing his books with highlighter, staying out late for lectures on "The American Imaginary," or "New Media Theory," or "Film and Myth," or "The Dialectics and Metaphysics of Filmic Techniques." After his first semester he began research for a respected professor. ("He tries very hard to be cinematic," Demetri said of this man. "Like he has a dove. He carries around a dove." I asked him what that meant. "Like"—he raised his brows and flapped his arms out wide*—"like a real-life dove. A dove. It's damaged or something.") Demetri was conspicuously present at all the film series events and was developing the program for next year. The student with the winning program would win the presidency of some club. Demetri wanted to win, but he was waiting to settle on an idea. ("I am not thinking exactly the way I want to be thinking," he had told me, keeping himself vague.)

I ran to meet him at the café and only said: "Let's go."

"Where?"

**Wide*, acrylic on unprimed cotton canvas, medium
Can't explain. A luxurious sense of stretch in this one. Kinetic, too, like you're snapping inside yourself.

"Out. Or insane."

He reminded me about his date with Rose. I told him I would wait for him there at the café as he went and finished with her.

"Are you serious?" He raised his brow in a way that suggested I shouldn't be.

"Yes."

He left. I sat alone for a while. A young couple came in. They sat in a booth. Two babysitters came in with their small clients. I wanted to ask them—I wanted to ask everyone—if they recognized me. I was sure deep down that they must.

Demetri had left his coffee on the table. He'd only taken a sip. He was experimenting with being extremely caffeinated at all times, as if this would produce intellectual rigor. I watched the coffee ripple in his cup and realized I was shaking against the table. The hollow at my center gained control. I searched for a pencil. On the back of the menu, I began to sketch without intention. Rose appeared, first her tiny face, then her dull almond eyes, then her blooming brown curls. And then Demetri, beside her, feeding the newspaper into her terrorized little mouth. I sketched fast, feeling myself turn dumb, or dense, in that meditative way.

I calmed down. I placed the sketch in my bag. My plan was to work in Demetri's dorm and then go out. I'd lie out on the grass and pride myself on what I imagined might be my unique trajectory. I'd look for cock formations in the sky, take my pants off and pretend I was being fucked by the universe. I'd laugh at myself. I'd find a drunk frat boy to take to the bushes. I'd lay him down naked and paint him his ass crack—which, if he asked, I'd explain as a small fissure in the vast body of the universe, which technically it was.

But Demetri, to my surprise, was in his room. I heard him through the closed door. He was with Rose, whose voice was little. I looked again at my sketch. I did not realize it was so rich with gore. Rose's veins drawn with macabre girth. I slipped the doodle under his door and waited. I listened as Demetri tried to calm her down. "My sister," he kept saying. "And it's really not even her best." He tried to reassure her, to laugh. He could sense me outside the door, which never opened, and I knew he was thinking of my portrait of Willow, which in the end he'd declared "actually looked nothing like her."

I slept on the couch in the lounge. I didn't complain. When he at last allowed me in, I tried to apologize. We were silent. Finally, I asked him about his film program, if he managed to come up with something and finish it.

"Not yet." He looked hard at the floor. "I'm trying to make it very big," he said. "I'll figure it out."

I took the newspaper off his desk. It was open to the page with my images. I asked him if he thought he'd make it as big as me.

"Bigger," he said. "So big you'll miss me."

And he was right, I thought. I could keep pushing him because he was going to make it. There is no way to overstate my belief in his ascendance. I believed it with the force of a society, the way a country understands the right of an heir. It was what I had been told. He would exceed me but would not forget that once—or maybe twice—I had won.

My final push came in the form of a self-portrait. Zara led me to a bulletin board, where among flyers about upcoming club meetings and tutor availability and blow jobs, there was a notice about a self-portrait competition. "A lot of money," was all she said as she unpinned the paper and gave it to me. The portrait could be in any medium and of any size—it could be abstract or realist, physical or digital. The prize money was $5,000. The winner was to be judged by a board of graduate students and professors. Zara made no reference to the one prohibitive criterion, written in red, which was that the submitter must currently be attending Harvard as an undergraduate.

"You know that I'm not, yes?"

Zara shrugged. I asked her why she wouldn't enter.

"I'm already rich." She tilted her head back and spread her arms apart, a summons of mania. "I'm *fat* and rich. You're poor, and I think maybe dying."

It's true Demetri and I were having a difficult time. I'd gotten to know and disarm the guards who stood at his building, but I could not get into the dining hall, guarded hard by the impenetrable lunch-lady bureaucracy. At my request Demetri sometimes brought me food—meatballs disintegrated in napkins, pocketfuls of cereal, brownies molded to the shape of his thigh. But more than food, I needed books. The thick anthology of art Zara showed me called *Graphic Gateway* contained instructions on basic designs and the fundamentals of sketching. Each time I looked at it I thought of others having a large meal without me. My most pressing concern was that my colored pencils—good ones, thirty dollars a box—were beginning to nub. Demetri did not know these things because I did not mention them. When our father's every-so-often checks arrived we bought Demetri new Moleskines, Montblanc fountain pens, Post-its.

"I have to enter," I told Demetri. We were sipping hot coffee through tiny red straws, sitting at the new café near the library, the fancy one with high-backed booths upholstered in purple velvet. Vomit stains crisped up the fabric.

Demetri—wearing black slacks and a dark purple turtleneck, dressed up for a simulation*—sat there with an air of overcomposure and said no, I could not enter. They would need proof I was a student. That was "literally the only requirement," he said, and under no circumstances did I meet it.

"Demetri." I watched his teeth wilt his straw. "I obvi-

**Simulation*, oil on linen, small
I painted this in a deep purple and with a tiny, tiny, tiny brush. Micro lines. Hated it as it was coming out. Hate it now.

ously don't mean a portrait of me. I mean a portrait of you."

I waited to see how long it would take him.

"Meaning," I went on, "that I create a portrait of you, and you submit it as your own, as something you made, but we call it a self-portrait, and we get the money."

"But everyone knows I don't paint." He pulled his straw halfway out of his cup. Pushed it back in. Pulled it out.

"No one really knows you at all." Although I thought of Zara calling him *this boy*.

He considered this. "But I don't look like a painter."

"How does a painter look?"

"Like you," he said, assessing me.

"But you *do* look like me."

He looked away. "On bad days."

"Which you are always having."

He paused. "What if they find out?"

I told him I didn't know what they would do. They would take back the prize money. I didn't know what else.

"Five thousand dollars . . ." Demetri said. "That's not that much money."

I said it was more than we had ever heard of, in relationship to ourselves.

"Yes," he said. Then he looked at me like he had two more pairs of eyes tucked* beneath the first. "You want to

---

**Tucked*, acrylic on unprimed cotton canvas, large

have your talent tested," he said. "You want to win among the trained." He looked as if this was his first time considering the possibility.

"Of course that's true."

He nodded. Like this discovery was monumental but he'd take it with mature resignation. "Fine," he said. I waited. "Yes, fine, you can do it."

I asked him if he was sure.

"Yes, fine. I also want to see if you win." His eyes were testing.

"As long as I don't lose," I said, "and you end up frustrated with yourself."

"Never myself. Only with you." He used two fingers to pull at the fabric at his neck. "But do what you like."

Sitting with him I wondered if I had intentionally tempted him to admit to me—when I said that we looked alike—that no, we did not look alike, because by any objective measure he was attractive and I was not. That was our main difference. But no, Demetri did not think in those terms. Questions of beauty did not enhance him or distract him or casually destroy him, and that he had grown so immune, in his own way, was of course the deeper difference.

Two weeks later, a week before the portrait was due,

Tucked (cont.): Sometimes I try to give this look to people and I'm pretty sure I just look constipated.

Demetri came home and told me he had reversed his decision. I was not to draw him, I was not to submit.

He had fallen in love—he used the term—with a real woman. Erica, a graduate student five years his senior who he met at a public reading by a psychology professor. They'd bonded over choosing orange as their favorite fruit when taking part in an experiment, something about one's inclination to eat the colors of one's energy. Orange meant energetic. "And she is," he told me. "She's got excessive energy. She wears special polish so she doesn't bite her nails. She's getting a PhD in art history. And she's on that board," he said, whipping a blanket over his bed. "The one that's choosing the portraits. So no more of that." He ran his fingers through his hair and did not look at me.

To Demetri's credit, he and Erica really did go out. I knew this mostly because I was aware of the money Demetri was spending on items having nothing to do with either of us. He thought the relationship was serious. And I could sense—in the way he walked around, ate, slept—that his seriousness was part of his larger mood, which revealed itself in smaller gestures, all of which he tracked: How many times in a day did he remake his bed? At what rate did he pace desk to door to desk to door? It was a Demetri mood in which every moment of living could be measured by the presumed impact of that moment on the course of the rest of his life. He began timing himself walking up the stairs.

He could not imagine sacrificing a moment of serious intention with one of frivolity, and he was not going to believe anyone else would ever do such a thing, either.

He believed Erica, for instance, was committed to him. When he spoke of her it was with a sense of future—a sense of anticipated time that he knew she'd fill up. And he needed someone to fill up his time because he hadn't decided on anything—no definite direction. We were waiting for him. As he walked around I could feel him reminding himself of his successes. The first of which, he thought, was having any potential at all. "I know that whatever I do," he told me, "it will be big and rare." He had no embarrassment about expecting the best of himself. He expected everyone to be so committed to themselves, and so was unwittingly committed to misunderstanding people. Everything he looked at, read, watched, observed, all of it consumed with a very particular end in mind. That he could think only in terms of utility meant he consistently obstructed what was of actual use: the gradual, semiconscious accumulation of impressions, a relaxed thickening of the imaginative network. I watched him walk around having no idea that his desire for ambition was—by my standards at least—thinning his experience of life.

When I met Erica (or rather when I heard her speak to Demetri from my position outside his door) I knew she was his equal, and I knew my brother did not know it. She was only playing, flirting with seriousness rather than engaging with it. She was not going to commit, nor should she. I expected Demetri to understand this.

"Yes, you're cute," I heard her say through the door. Then their whispers. Then laughter. "Am I your Phaedra?"

"My favorite?" His voice was high. (Demetri was never more womanly than when pursuing a woman.)

"Your Phaedra," she said.

"Phaedra?"

I heard her take a step back. There was a smokiness in her voice which I immediately found addictive. "From Euripides," she said. "Phaedra, the older queen, falls in love with her husband's son, Hippolytus. Basically like her stepson. I basically just mean I'm a cougar." She laughed.

"Oh—" Demetri was giddy at having his life likened to tragedy. "Yes yes yes!"

"They both die, Demetri," Erica added. "Phaedra and Hippolytus." She laughed again.

I heard it as a warning—she and Demetri would not last. Demetri understood it as a sealing of their fate, a recognition that together, at some point, they would enter eternity. After this I heard silence between them.

"So hairy," she suddenly said.

"I know."

"Why so hairy?"

"It's from my sister," he said.

"A gift?" She laughed.

He explained to her that when he was little, I rubbed a

stick of butter over his calves and, stealing a razor from our mother, shaved him ankle to thigh. (We got the idea from watching her in the bathtub as she made shaving cream disappear in these long, shining streaks up her legs. When I finished with the razor we held the blade to the light—it looked stuffed with bug legs. We pulled out the hairs and rolled them between our fingers, and then took the rest of the butter and used it to fry ourselves eggs, the yellow yolks bright* like Demetri's knees.) The hair grew back, of course, thickened from the blunted tip, and darker from who knows.

"So that's very weird," Erica said. "And just not what I was expecting like at all. I kind of *fucking* love it." Erica asked if she could shave him again. "There's just something perversely ritualistic about it?" she said. "And I'm interested in that. I'm thinking about Herodotus and the Egyptian priests. How their bodies were shaved by slaves with these amazing jewel-encrusted razors. They took everything off. Like even eyelashes. They were extreme." She was being erotic.

Demetri did not want to be shaved. He was self-conscious about the hair already, how thick it was. ("When I try to touch my toes, I suffocate.")

**Bright*, oil on canvas with ground glass, medium
Only because I still had some glass left over from *Crystallizing* and needed some brightness, which really works over the bright yolk yellow. This one is beautiful.

"Okay," he said. I heard her whisper as she sprayed the cream.

That night I confessed to Demetri that I submitted him—a portrait of him—to the competition. I told him I'd been painting him in his sleep. I said again we needed the money. I knew that eventually he'd make the rest of it, but that I had to do one thing for us right now, and all he had to say was that he painted it. He could say I taught him how. When he paused what he was doing—when he looked at me and tilted his neck forward, without moving the rest of his body—I knew something else was coming. And then he lifted the dictionary at the corner of his desk and threw it at me. Hard, where I saw his lips pull back* with effort. The instant it was thrown I knew it would not hit me. I knew it was not meant to. I thought of moving so that maybe it would, so I could at least be the victim of something.

Later the same evening, he was lying on his bed, three feet above me. "It's not something I want to discuss," he said. He'd told Erica they could no longer see one another. It was impossible. The risk was too high. She, as one of the judges, would see the portrait and know his deceit. And when she charged him with it, he'd have to confess.

I was trying to be kind then and used the softest voice I

**Pull back*, oil and tempera on Claybord, small
Painting with tempera is never a good idea.

had. "I still don't understand," I said. "Do you see why it's a little absurd to me? You think Erica would just assume you couldn't have painted this portrait of yourself?"

"Yes."

"Demetri."

"How can you not understand?" His voice was flat.

"Why can't you tell me? I'm not trying to be dumb. You really could have done it. I want to understand." With my mattress stationed beneath his, I was grateful not to have to look at him.

He took a moment. "Your understanding would somehow be more painful than your not understanding."

"Then I promise not to understand."

"Because," he said, after a long minute, "I meant what I said before. I don't look like an artist in that way. Or it's not even the look. I just mean I just don't seem like I'd be capable. I mean the lie wouldn't work. She wouldn't believe I made it. She knows I can't see myself like that. I know that and it's really fine. I've resigned myself."

I told Demetri that even if this natural incapacity of his was true—which it was, and I liked that he thought so—he gave Erica too much credit. Why couldn't she be fooled into thinking he made it? Why did he think she saw some inartistic quality in him that would make him *incapable* of a portrait like mine? I said she was smart, but that wasn't her type of insight. She wasn't interested in the ways in which people saw themselves.

"You're wrong. She sees things. She knows a lot about herself."

I said she did seem to be very good at perceiving herself, but that this was a limit, not a measure by which we might judge her other insights.

Demetri sighed. "That you just make the choice not to like certain people—"

"You think I have a choice!"

Demetri was silent. Then: "And then there's the other reason, which is, why would anyone present themselves like that?"

"What do you mean 'like that'?"

"So weak like that."

"How weak?"

"That's the only way you do me."

I spun to the edge of my mattress. "You didn't even look at it!" It's true. By then, he'd refused to see what I made of him, just as I'd go on to refuse to see any film he worked on.

"Because I know what you do to me. It gets exhausting. I don't even like the idea."

"What idea?"

"Of the contest. Of the self-portrait."

"You don't even like the idea of the self-portrait?" I squinted, trying to pull names from Zara's book. "Dürer, Rembrandt, Kahlo . . ."

"That's not what I mean. None of those people look weak in theirs." He paused; I felt his feet above me. "If they seem weak it's not real weakness. There's a pride there that knows its weakness. You make me look like I have no *fucking* idea how weak I am. You just make me weak-weak. Just weak."

"I really think you're confused." I told Demetri that the only reason he saw confidence in those self-portraits was because he was aware, when looking at them, that the painters had done them themselves. "And so *other* people who *think* you made it will see in it all the same qualities that you see in those ones. They'll project all of that onto it. You won't seem weak to them."

"So I'll seem weak only to myself," he said.

"Yes."

"And to you."

"Exactly."

"You're being cruel, Ava."

"You're asking me to!"

"You've missed the point," he said. I started to restate something. "We don't have to talk anymore."

An hour passes. I am sure he is asleep. Until I hear him above me: "And I know," he begins and then clears his throat. "I know that you hate me for being so fucking serious all the fucking time. But you can't hate that about me more than I hate it in myself. It's killing me. So don't worry."

The next week, when we received the notice that we'd won, Demetri expressed no emotion. There was a small reception. Demetri was brought onstage. A check was written in his name, and he said thank you, red-faced and quiet, into the microphone. Zara stood next to me in the back of the room. She was there to report on the winner. But when Demetri heard her clicking her camera, when he saw me standing there beside her, looking who knows what way, he—after one long sigh—began to emit a series of sounds. I thought he was only mumbling, that maybe he'd tripped into the microphone. Until I heard him: "Wait." He bent forward and lifted the portrait up next to his face and said, "It's not me." The crowd, which had already applauded, did not hear him. "It's not me," Demetri said again. "I didn't do it, and it's not me. It's not me. It's not me." He paused again. The audience went quiet. He began to laugh. "No, it's really not me. It's not me . . ." More silence. The audience all turned inward, toward one another. He laughed again, looked disbelieving. "Hi," he said. Still, nothing. "Okay." I knew he would say no more. No one was going to question him. The sensitive artist's natural disinclination toward public exposure, they thought. A natural volatility; a productive alienation from the self. They paid almost no attention. I stood there and did not laugh. Demetri looked at me and then looked away. He'd confessed, he thought, and his conscience was clear. He could take the money—and he did—though he did not shake the hand of the committee director, which for the man was a rebuff, but which for Demetri, I knew, was some kind of preservation of honor.

A day or so later Erica wrote him a note. *I knew you were complicated*, was how it began. She didn't know why he had stopped seeing her, but it was clear from both the portrait and his speech at the ceremony that his internal life would always elude her. When Demetri left the room, I read the rest of the note, which was full of inaccurate but deeply felt insights. She should have known—for example—that when he blinked at her in quick succession, he wasn't coming up with feelings to express but instead could not choose between them. She should have known he stood in shadows when he was in a good mood, trying to maintain its warmth. No wonder he succeeds and denies it. *You are confounding*, she wrote. *You exist according to a code that hasn't been established.* She mistook his confusion for complexity. I imagined she'd go on to tell her future lovers that she was once with a boy too deep to ever know. In a way, I felt proud for helping to serve this fantasy.

Things are shifting up here in my apartment. It's getting colder. The air outside has turned purple and pale. I am sure that right about now there are lovers relaxing down by the Hudson River, sprawled out on the grass, tote bags with sandwiches and a bottle of sparkling water inside. I've thought about being this kind of person. The kind who lets time pass without asking for anything in return. If Demetri and I have anything in common it is the inability to do just this. After graduating Demetri wanted to travel. He wanted to teach English over in Italy or maybe China and learn to sail and fish and wear those linen shirts that look good on boats. To be someone for whom death becomes increasingly less threatening as you wade deeper into equilibrium.

Instead, we moved to New York. He moved into a studio apartment with a large closet and a bathroom with ash-pink tiles. He set to real work. He began digging up archival material for a small documentary studio—materials for their digital advertisements for films about past eras and all their plagues and all their triumphs. He hated this work, but pretended the cursory encounters with old images were making him smarter. "I am learning," he'd tell me, "thinking in sepia. It is enriching."

I began to think he'd lost interest in making things of his own, when at once he announced to me: "The NEA. The National Endowment for the Arts. I'm going to submit an idea. I looked it up . . ."

He's bright. It's four years since he graduated, and we're on a bench near my new apartment on Eighth Avenue and Fifteenth Street. I pay my first six months' rent with the commission that I'd made on four sales of my work: First, the *LiveStreaming* series, whose $15,000 sale made us go mute for two days. Then a grid of my early nudes, which was featured on a bidding platform called Inside Artists and sold for a not-embarrassing $9,000; then the untitled Harvard boys series, sold to a male professor under the condition of anonymity for $3,000; and lastly a grid of my abstract assholes, which surprisingly sold for $9,000 after being placed in an exhibition titled *Modern Void.* Demetri coordinated the sales, found ways to organize the work, started various accounts, and obtained certain copyrights. He dealt with shipment, taxes. After paying rent, I had $116 left over each month. Just under four dollars per day. One-off sales and other commissions helped with week-to-week foodstuffs. If no commissions came in, I would put up a huge poster of my face with my phone number in my building's lobby, asking to be paid to watch people's children. Or I'd message local shops asking if they needed design assistance to create a logo—I was good for a vibrant revamp. I considered going into advertising before realizing the artists who ended up there would be suicidal with the exact same casualness as me.

At the park, sitting next to Demetri, the new wooden bench boards press hard against my ass. The woman across from us has three small dogs on her lap, looks kind of fancy in a snakeskin dress, and keeps screaming at me that I'm a dork, and it's making Demetri laugh. It's an image of him I'd have liked to sketch, but after winning the competition Demetri's face was forever off-limits to me. I swore this to him.

"You are pitching the NEA—the nation? For funding?" I ask.

He nods.

"What's the idea?"

"I'm going to make a documentary. I mean a film." Demetri looks over at his leather lace-ups, which are not on his feet because of a violent* pair of blisters.

"I thought you were about to be paid to do that." He was sure he'd soon be promoted from working on promotional material to working on the documentaries themselves.

"Yes. But my own. I mean about us."

**Violent*, watercolor on tissue paper, small
Violent blisters can also look like a sunrise over a mesa, or an inflamed organ, as you'll see.

I wait to see if he might be joking. "You're going to document me?"

"Well, not *you*." He looks straight ahead. "I just mean it's a good topic for me, because first, I know it, and also because I can experiment. No one is going to tell me how to do it right. No one is going to say"—here he lifts his hands, points them this way and that—"'*Demetri*, this decade needs more texture' or 'the victims need more depth' or 'it's this way and not that way.' I mean, it'd be a kind of freedom. I've been looking for something." He looks at me. I can't tell what he wants me to think.

"Demetri," I shake my head.

"What?"

I keep shaking my head no.

"Why?" He lifts a shoelace with his toes.

"That's too much."

"But there's footage." I'm going to ask where, but I remember our father filming us when we were younger, the birthday interviews, how Demetri would answer our father's questions but often I would not react. I ask him if that's the footage he means. "Yes," he says. "Partially. It's the right time. Enough people care about you now."

"No one cares," I say, and mean it.

"Well, they might start to. In a sense I was only waiting for enough people to care. And so maybe that's why I made it happen." He means my projects.

"Nothing has really happened," I say. We'd agreed my three larger sales were a kind of dumb luck.

"But it will happen," he says. "And I gave you what you needed for it, and you became it, or are becoming it or will become it. And now I'm going to become it, because you'll give it back to me and so we'll both have it. No?"

Again I nod no. I tell him I'm afraid to take him seriously.

"I'm not joking. I would do it perfectly."

I ask him: "But what if you make it and then nothing actually becomes of me?"

"You don't understand. Nothing would have to become of you. It would be great on its own terms. As a piece of art on its own terms."

"Something would have to become of me," I say, "to prove it was worth making."

"Ava this isn't about you, if you're listening."

"It is literally going to be about me, I thought."

"Not all of it."

I scoot to the edge of the bench and try to understand what exactly I'm rebelling against. It takes me some time. Demetri sits and waits.

Soon he laughs. "I cannot just be alive and not be able to do anything."

I look down at his feet, the pink at his heel. And suddenly I picture Demetri sprinting around our childhood block. He had wanted to play football. He made it onto the team. But he was often so late to practice that he'd have to sprint up the hill in his gear to make it on time, and then was so bad at football that—having learned to sprint—they moved him to track. "Even when I try to make a decision for myself," he goes on, "it doesn't work."

"You're not *not* doing anything, Demetri."

"You're not being clear. You've already prostituted yourself and your life," he says. "If that's what you're worried about. Is that not what you're doing? You've told me. Everything we've been is in there, in whatever you're making in there." He points up to my building. "Is mine different?" Wind bisects his bangs down the middle. His face is so symmetric that he looks pasted* together. I can tell he's trying very hard not to be dramatic. I suddenly feel embarrassed. My stomach drops a little.

"Don't listen to me. I don't know what I just said. But I'm just saying no."

"I'm not asking for permission."

"You brought it up as a question."

"Ava. I need to find out new things about myself. I'm getting severely bored with myself . . . I need to find out new things."

"You don't rehearse your past to find them!" I'm yelling. "Just live differently!"

**Pasted*, pencil, crayon, and synthetic polymer paint on paper, medium
Like when you are in a bathroom with many mirrors, and in a certain corner you can align the same side of your face to make one whole face, and it is so wrong.

He leans his head back. His neck stretches tight over veins. Then he returns. "You don't think I'm capable of making something great, that will move people. You think I can't offer an experience." I am sickened and slightly relaxed by how true this might be. Then he tells me a story. He read, somewhere in a novel, about a famous writer who—before she became a writer—desperately wanted to be a musician. "A pianist. She was convinced it would happen. She'd release a studio album. She'd blow up. She thought this until the very day she gave her piano away. She gave it away because she realized that she was an excellent player, not a *brilliant* player—she was a pleasure to behold but not an *experience* to have. She had to get rid of the instrument. The slim margin of her failure—the distance between greatness and *genius*, slim but insuperable—it ruined her. But, of course, once the piano was gone, she was set free to write. And now we know her as a writer. That's her art."

"And?" I asked.

"I have to throw away my piano."

"And what's your piano?"

"Work." He looks at me. Curls limp on his forehead. "Working on other people's projects, this archival shit, working on other people's ideas for films or whatever."

I consider. "Work is everyone's piano."

"Yes. But you're not understanding," he says. Now we're both looking down, watching ants gather over a blueberry. "My work is extra piano. Because of exactly how tangentially related it is to what I really want to do." He sits up. "You know the famous thing about how weathermen want to be stand-ups, how pilots want to be birds." He's flipping his hand higher toward the sky.

I try to be as honest as possible and tell him that the assumption anyone would care about our life embarrasses me. That documentary would be too literal an expression. It would not work. And then, in the way he looks at me, I realize I might be ruining something. "But we'll get you to own something else," I say. "In fact, I brought you this." I take from my tote a small sketch of a dog. It's from a series called *Getting to Know the Neighbor*—a collection of forty-seven portraits of every resident in my building, made soon after I moved in. (I stood behind the doorman's desk and sketched the security footage—captured the residents walking in, fetching their mail, entering the elevator. I did it simply because I have an addiction to the way people move in these private, public spaces. Demetri ended up writing the release for me; he titled the series *The Watchman* and said I was "an artist who took modern themes of surveillance seriously." The critics bought it. They echoed his sentiments. I knew the way in which "every building now functions as a rectilinear panopticon." The work would get me a temporary spot in a midlevel gallery. It would sell in large lots. I didn't know this at the time.)

On the bench, Demetri takes the portrait from me. "What is it?"

"Tadzio." The dog, also a resident, with whom Demi has an intense mutual affection. Tadzio was not included in the series because I was embarrassed at not getting his hair right. The strands were too fine.

"You're giving me a dog. And still saying no."

"I am saying no." I'm not able to look at him. "I am saying no, I am not to be the subject of your work. Not me." I want to get his guarantee that he won't begin. I want him never to ask me why I would not trust his sensibility, because I would not have an answer. The sun starts going down, and when I look at him the light is hardening his eyes. The temperature drops the way spring lets it. We go home.

NATI IS ABOUT TO ENTER. Everything will shift. Demetri himself was already shifting. These are the months where we rail at each other. Neither of us thinks the other is doing it—anything—right. For reasons that are beyond us, we do not encourage one another. I project onto him my own fear of my premature obsolescence. This is when I show up on his block in my leotard. This is when Demetri tells me I have to give up portraiture altogether because I am not capturing people correctly. He tells me to go back to the plants I drew when we were children. Back to basics. He says this right as I am commissioned to paint a double portrait of a Japanese billionaire and her half-Kenyan son. The woman calls me after seeing my surveillance portraits.

She asks if she and her son might pose for me together in her apartment. I agree. I arrive at her penthouse—five bedrooms, lofted ceilings, wood everywhere. Slim oak trimming along the walls and door frames—all of it polished, to show off its rusticity. "From a church in the Subcarpathian region," the woman tells me. "And this, from the Meiji period," she says, pointing to a massive model pagoda, three-tiered, built with slender cherry wood pillars and miniature balustrades, mahogany Buddhas squat in every corner.

The woman's son is seventeen. When I arrive, he's already posed in the den. He is young but stands with a strong and convincing presence. His chest is tight under his skin. There's a low light running through his center body.

His mother knows his beauty. She doesn't acknowledge it. When she stands to pose with him, she doesn't look at him. His entire being is a phantom limb for her, which she can exercise without ever addressing directly. The portrait, she tells me, is for her husband, the boy's father, whom she has recently divorced, whom she wants to make jealous, and in whose eyes, she says, she wants to be seen as multidimensional.

I paint it all wrong. The woman wants her hand up and out, so I have to foreshorten. I'm still not good at this. Demetri gives me Caravaggio, Michelangelo. But then my colors are too thick from all my attempts. The painting looks embarrassed to be realist, but also lacks the intelligence to make some abstract comment. I tell the woman it is a first draft. I am so pent up with feeling that I give the portrait to the building's porter who rides the elevator down with me—a young man with a tattoo of a cross on his middle finger. He says he won't take it. "Maybe it's a breach of something," he says, blinking out his nerves. I stand with him and begin pulsing. I look at the pores drilled deep into his skin. I convince him right then to fuck me down in the building's basement, where there's a parking garage. Minutes later, when he's inside me, I think only of the boy I failed to get on a canvas, his body and his unsettling submission to his mother. I tell Demetri all of this. He says I've probably violated something. I tell mother and son that I can't come back.

"You know, people are not meant to be seen, really," Demetri explains to me.

It's only a week after my portrait failure and I am still raw. Demetri is in a confessional mood. He is lying on my kitchen floor. (Sitting here now, writing on my stool, I turn my head and see the exact patch of wood where he lay, his feet up against the dishwasher.) "It's probably not good to be seen so completely, for so long. People are supposed to show you their spirit in one ecstatic flash and then cycle back into their own plane. If you're going to paint, you have to capture that. I don't know how to do it, so I can't tell you," he says. I see his legs lift across the floor from me. "I know how you work. You only want control. Your way about it is wrong. There are more mysterious ways of controlling things."

"Please find out," I say.

"I feel like you're in need of a certain ethics. Like how there's an ethics of care or an ethics of ambiguity or of this or that."

"Or maybe," I say, not meaning it, "I'm just not painting the right people."

"Maybe," Demetri says. "Maybe it's something else. Maybe it's really, really bad. Worse than we can think. Maybe everyone's just dead."

I don't answer. Demetri does not think anyone is dead. We were just on the bus. He sighed loudly in his usual fashion and then made a general comment about the heat—"I'm twisting on a spit"—to attract conversation. He and an older man were wearing matching shoes. They talked about boils. "Gotta get it moist before it drains." Before we got off he made eyes with a group of sweating nannies. He nodded wisely like he knew the deal.

"Everyone is dead," he continues. "Still I'm trying for some fun. I've started engaging in illicit activities."

"Like?"

He hands me his phone. "I'm sending my photos to men."

I look through the photos. Timed selfies of Demetri seated with his head in his hands; Demetri standing on his tippy-toes in his kitchen. Demetri at a bookstore.

"Demetri, these are not illicit."

"Yes, but what the men do with them . . . They're used for illicit stuff."

"Like what?"

"I don't know. It's illicit." He's smiling. He waits. "And I've been becoming very interested in sports, too. And now I'm addicted to watching people's muscle-gain journeys online," he says. "I like watching people grow, matter getting added to things. I like watching people eat. And the filming of the food. Close-ups of pasta in a colander shaken like lard. Close-ups of curdles in an omelet. The milk-yellows, the mood music." He taps my floor with his fingers. "You'd like it, maybe."

We don't mention the fact that he is lonely. That, still, his pragmatism and code of restraint cannot accommodate what he wants to feel. In this time, he nevertheless has girlfriends. On the floor he tells me about Aleni, his latest.

"Her parents' house—I went, by accident." He turns to look at me, raising his brows so they're halfway up his forehead. "It was a mistake. The father is a professor. And his library is this massive room, a big oak lodge, basically. I noticed five sets of encyclopedias. I asked him what the differences were between them and he said he had never opened them. And there was a taxidermied snake curling out of the wall. He saw me notice the snake—named Bo—and made me put my head through the coil and then made sounds like he was inhaling me. He's very kind and insane.

Anyway, Aleni took me on her family's boat. They were throwing a party for something. And so there was a dinner and there were waiters on the boat. And Aleni was so nice to the waiters and made a point to show me she knew all about the waiters' children and their wives. She looked at them so long, like she could never tire of knowing them or of hearing about them. And I wanted to fall in love with her. But I couldn't. It was all too nice. Her parents are really nice. Very even people. Really nice. Really, really nice. I don't think it'd work. I don't think we'd be asking ourselves the same questions in our life."

"What questions are you asking?" I lift off the floor and sit cross-legged.

"I don't know. Probably that's my problem. I have no central question. I only have these dreams, all of other women. I'm forced into romantic treason. My dreams are of other things and of a totally other life. In real life I'm just, deceiving. I don't know." I try to interrupt him. "And then for that reason"—he lifts his hands over his head—"I know I am always approaching life and never living it. Always only approaching it. Because I don't really know what it is . . ."

"Demetri," I remind him, "you are at your best when you are indifferent to yourself."

"No, I know. And Aleni, anyway," he says, pretending not to hear me, "she is the kind who likes to analyze. So she'd make things worse. I'm saying it wouldn't work. Plus, she wouldn't lie to me. Which would be a huge issue. There'd come a time where I wouldn't want to know what she really thought of me. But she'd tell me and tell me and tell me."

He's in this state of mind when we at last go to Italy.

After the Virgin Islands trip, we'd never left the mainland. Leaving was something for other people to do. But suddenly it feels necessary. Demetri is turning twenty-nine. He feels nothing has happened or is happening to him. He needs to leave New York. I pay for it. I have the exact amount of money left over from a sale. Two round-trip flights, each flight a red-eye with two connections. We don't care. We decide where to go: there's the pull toward Tuscany—the water—but we end up in Rome. Demetri has a friend there, Lena, who reports on the Rome-based auction houses. She lets us stay with her in what is both the darkest and most visually pleasing apartment I've been in. On Via di San Salvatore. I can still smell her lacework curtains hiding the view of a brick wall.

At night Lena takes us to a huge churchyard. The church itself has already been demolished. "Tomorrow, they break new ground." She tells us they'll be building an arts center. And, to celebrate, a party's going on.

It's midnight and the yard is sprawling with Italian bodies, dancing and chatting over black-green grass. Dancing figures peeled off a Roman vase and come to life. An Italian band sings acoustic versions of American pop. Their instruments glow amber and all around it smells like blown-out flames.

I'm standing against a cast-iron fence, talking to Demetri. He's in a thick-weave button-down the color of stone. I watch him notice someone behind me. I already know who it is. I saw her come in. Tall. An insolent angle to her face. Without turning to confirm, I watch his eyes move at the pace of her body. I see him seeing her black hair. Her odd beauty is laid across his face, taking him beyond the realm of understanding. His eyes are free, fearful.*

"Demi, what were you telling me?"

"Hold on."

I watch him go to her. She's talking to someone. He waits for their conversation to end and then introduces himself—he's smiling and looking down. I watch her lean body. Her response is warm. She puts her hair behind her ears. He takes it like it's given to him when her earring falls out, landing in a mess of hair above her shoulder. She throws her neck back at the idea of having lost something. Her laughter is hearty and comes through the dust as something thick and archaic.

"Demetri." I hear her repeat his name to him as she puts the hoop back in.

"Ava's brother." He's laughing.

Nati (though I've yet to learn her name) looks toward me. She finds me watching them, and when our eyes meet

---

**Fearful*, acrylic on small ceramic plate
Painted this on a plate because I ran out of other material.

the hook into her is sharp. I have no idea that she saw my trite mugs at Harvard, when she was there following some other talent. I don't know that she knows my name, or that she's been tracking me, watching my progress. That night she looks away from me, says something to Demetri—and I'm looking too carefully at her mouth to understand what it is. I watch Demetri gesture toward the demolished church. I'm sure that he is saying something about the era in which it was originally built. Something statistical—I can tell by the way Nati nods like she's accommodating a fact. She likes Demetri. She puts her hand on him and laughs again.

In the cab back to Lena's we pass fountains that sprout what looks like black ink, up into clouds of deep clay. We're leaving the next day. In the cab Demetri looks out the window. He slams his hands on his thighs. "It's full tonight." He points up. "Constellations. Ursa Major. Ursa Minor." He sneezes three times, points at himself. "Sinus Congestus."

A MONTH LATER Demetri still has not brought her up.

SOON WE'RE SUPPOSED to go to a reception. I ask him if he wants to bring Aleni. He says no. He's thinking of Nati—the fact that he has not brought her up proves it.

The reception is, in part, for me. I won third (which is to say last) place in a young artists competition. The competition acknowledged my success with the use of some grant money. I had listened to Demetri. I'd gotten away from humans and made portraits of other entities. My *Material Potatoes* were what earned me the prize—each potato made out of a smattering of materials (a couple from papier-mâché, wire, glitter, rock; others made from Bakelite and glass). For two weeks, the potatoes were on public view in the subway stations. Then they moved temporarily to an up-and-coming gallery. All the pieces sold. It was written—by Demetri, but this time by others, too—that I had "a flair for the hairy, the odd." I gave "an exuberance, a new life, to what was quintessentially gray, ugly, and earthy." People found the potatoes vain, maybe even haughty. Others called me the new eco-artist: I was aware of the soil. Of the violence man inflicted when he broke the earth open. I was restoring dignity to an abused object. Demetri had critiques he did not voice—despite writing the copy. By then we were a team. People took his presence with me as a given. If I was alone, I offered diminishing returns. If I was with him, or presented by him, there was interest.

To the reception I wear a sheer, hot-pink tube dress that makes me look like an electro–sausage link. Demetri wears a polo and a pair of jeans that cut off too early at the ankle. The party is in a grand room with a dome ceiling and sweeping marble floors. "And Ava"—I'm staring up at the ceiling, trimmed with neoclassical friezes—"Ava, Ava, what about you? You're ready to have first place next time?" The man who asks me this is short and carefully put together. Two little legs that whittle into almost nothing, then surprise you by landing in huge, splayed feet. I should probably recognize him. "What's next for you?" He is smirking.

You, I want to say. I'd like to paint you bent over, spread out. I'll fuck you for it. (Events make me aggressive.) Really, I am waiting for Demetri to come in and answer the question, but he is distracted, looking around. A man nearby is tsk-tsking. A lady's End Times laughter. Someone else has an accent. Demetri is trying to listen.

"Am I ready? Oh yes," I say.

"Oh yes!" The man repeats me. "Oh, you'll win it, you'll win it. How old are you?"

Demetri snaps back to attention. "Twenty-nine," he says.

"Twenty-eight," I say.

"Twenty-eight. So you have more than enough time." The man's feet rock him back and forth. He wears his smile like a wet hole in the head. I'm almost sure he's a critic.

"I would really much rather have less than enough time," I say. "Everything takes too long."

The man nods, approving, and begins to speak. Instead, Demetri again: "And by that, Ava means she enjoys constraints, creatively," he says. "I mean, not that she *creatively* enjoys the constraints but that she enjoys *creative* constraints. Although I suppose she *also* creatively enjoys those constraints. As opposed to unproductively enjoying them. You know." The man nods, is thoughtful, then makes a joke. Something about how I might become important. He makes another joke. Demi and I laugh again. But too hard, and for too long this time, both of us forgetting whose lead we are following. A senility is spreading between us. I watch the man grow suspicious. Demetri is now mimicking his rocking.

When the man walks away, I stand directly before Demetri. I feel the warm whir over his cheeks. Half-moons of light hinging his pupils.* "You're a little drunk," I laugh.

He shakes his head. "*You're* drunk."

"You," I say.

". . . areeeee"—he smiles—"drunk!"

We stand in a corner. People come by to congratulate me. I'm saying thank you when I hear Demetri: "Don't feel forced. Or, it's okay, you know, if you don't personally think it's great . . . talent . . ." he starts with someone. "And that kind of thing is understandable. I mean if you watch her work it's understandable. Painting is so funny. She puts a lot of paint on something. All of painting is breath. All of painting comes down to gathering little, itty-bitty commas. A big breath." He's laughing to himself. "A big sigh."

Another photographer comes by, takes our photo. Later, on the event's website, we're seen standing two inches

---

**Pupils*, oil on linen, medium
Please look at this one the longest.

apart. My hands are clasped over my crotch, nipples poking soft through hot-pink mesh. Demi's arms are loose by his sides. Just the week before, he'd officially been fired from his documentary company ("After eight years of the same shit, I began to lose focus," he told me. "I began to lose focus, and then I began even to lose focus on how terribly I'd lost focus"). He had taken to reckless smiling—here in the photograph it's an openmouthed, full-toothed grin.* Demetri gave the photographer our names. Ava and Demetri Stern. "That's *D* as in doodle, *E* as in . . . empty, or, *or*, every . . ."

In the cab home Demetri drums his hands on his legs. "Fun fun fun," he says. "And good food. Thick shrimp." He had cleared two trays of prawns. "Ava . . . Ava, did you think the think were shrimp? I mean the shrimp were think? I mean thick?"

The car slows. "*Think*," I say, enunciating. "*Thick. Think.*" I reach for my purse as Demetri continues to whisper the words. "So I guess," I say, "we pay now, but then I give the committee the receipt?" The prize committee was paying for our transportation.

"Yes, right." Demetri sits up. "We prow, pity on peats," he says, using his hands to help him through the sentence. I don't laugh. "I'm sorry. I was just funny because of before.

---

* ***Openmouthed, full-toothed grin***, graphite on paper, large
This was very hard.

Yes. Here." He takes too much cash from his wallet, burps, and tells the driver to keep it. "If we're being reimbursed . . ." He takes the receipt, puts it in his wallet. "Thank you, kind sir," he says, opening the door.

Once on the sidewalk, I sit him down on the stoop. He burps again. "What's next for you?" he says, peering at his hands. "Because you didn't answer the man."

"I was waiting for you to say it," I tell him.

"For me to say what's next for me?" We both know what I mean. "What project? Lots." He looks out over the banister. "I've been thinking."

"About?" I think he is going to say the documentary. It has not come up in three years, but ideas nestle and grow in him like disease.

Demetri burps again. "A girl."

"Oh? Which one?"

"No," he says. "I mean, I'm joking." I stand there and watch him and feel fully aware he is suffering. I do nothing about it.

He breathes deep and starts preparing, I know, not to list any women, but to give me a full list of ambitions, carefully considered goals, long-term projects. He's been taking notes over the past week on a new historical narrative project involving China and North Korea, making charts and saying things like *that's it* and punching his fist into his hand. On the stoop, I expect a lucid vision to erupt before him. Or for him to cave, to casually mention the unmentionable, which was that our mother would have just turned sixty. He opens his mouth, freezes for a minute, closes his mouth, holds his stomach, adjusts himself, and then vomits off the side of the stoop.

I stand, wait. He heaves again. A minute passes.

"Perfectly executed," I say, walking toward him. He moans. When he turns toward me a thread of drool is hanging thick* over his chin.

"Demi, wipe," I say. "Here." I point to my chin. He looks up at me, reaches out to wipe my face. "No," I laugh. "Not mine."

"Oh." I watch the thread take a new shape along his elbow. He smacks his lips, swallows. "Tastes acid," he said. "Acid shrimp." Cradling his head in his hands, he sighs again. I think more is coming, but he only sways, is silent—until, through his hands, sound. The words are slow, deliberate: "Thick . . . think. Thick. *Think*." He stops, spreads his fingers, finds my face, eyes white with moon.

The next week I'm supposed to go to Maine. There's a show there called *The Emerging*, and they have taken my *LiveStreaming* pieces. But I stay home. That night I walk into Demetri's apartment. He's not in the kitchen. I look

---

**Hanging thick*, texturized joint compound on canvas, large
Drool hanging thick catches the light in all kinds of weird ways.

toward the metal divider that separates his bed from the living space. The silence in the apartment deepens. I don't call for him.

I wind my way around the divider and find him in bed, lying down. I think he's under a newly purchased blanket. I look closer and make out a windowpane pattern. It's a dress. Our mother's. My first urge is to laugh, because I think he's put it on for me. But I remember I've come in unannounced—and that he is sleeping. I blink and try to get him out of my sight line. Demetri, I want to say. I know if he opens his eyes and it's not with laughter something horrible will have happened. I take two deep breaths to stop myself from making a sound. I back away.

There's a technique in painting where, to create the illusion of depth or corrosion, you repeatedly dab a sponge over a layer of wet paint. When the piece dries it looks like someone has scraped bits off the surface. Bone* shows through.

**Bone*, oil on linen, medium
I sponged on the wet painted bone and then used a toothbrush to further erode the edges.

I've stopped writing for a bit. It's dark now. Through my kitchen window I can see across the street into an elderly woman's bedroom. She's asleep but has left her lamp on. I like to stare out at her. On the pane of glass between us I see my own reflection, a specter. I stare at her real form through my reflected one. I open my mouth and arrange it so that her whole bed is inside me.

A week after the reception, Demetri wants to sit down for lunch. We choose our usual place, Awang, where the women like to talk to him about the hair on his knuckles ("like from a baby's head").

He sits on the linoleum chair across from me, sweating from the spices, and announces: "At certain dates in life you are to do certain things *with* your life."

I think he's talking about me. At this point, as far as my art is concerned, no one likes what I'm doing. Or, worse, no one cares, including myself. My most recent work was shown in a group exhibition titled *Chronos*. The theme was "new ways to register time." My piece was sculptural. I'd collected bits of hair from my own combs, shower drains at the gym, or anywhere public. I dried and then glued the hair together into long, wiry stalks. Then I arranged the stalks of hair so that they outlined shadow patterns cast throughout the day at the park on Seventh Avenue—the shadows at dawn, at noon, at dusk. I was trying to combine the idea of biological time—accumulated hair loss—and spatiotemporal time—sun, shadows. I am still seething from the sole review ("labored, trite") when Demetri, his mouth full of noodles, says: "I guess I'm thinking that right now you need, or maybe we both need, but mostly you need, I think, to find someone to fall in love with." This is how I know he is going to tell me about Nati. His elbows rest sharp on the table. "Where do you find someone like that?"

"To fall in love with?"

He nods yes, numb to the bits of chili on his lip.

"You go pick a girl from the line," I say, gesturing toward those standing and waiting for their takeout in a little parade of shifting weight. "Just go say hi."

Behind him a waiter opens a swing door. Briefly, I see inside the kitchen—two chefs are standing, one with his fingers in a bowl, the other studying a smoking pan. The door swings shut.

"I'm not just gonna go say hi," Demetri says.

I turn around. "She's cute." I'm nodding my head toward a young woman in jeans and a tunic, her brown hair up in a tortoiseshell clip. Fingers painted black. Medium-round tits. I look back at Demetri. His eyes match his shirt, gray and cottony. "You're afraid you'll expose yourself?"

"Yeah. And the wrong version of myself. The bolder version."

"The better one."

He nods and studies the splinters on his chopstick. "Yes. I've thought about doing that—about just talking to a person in a line, random like that. But the issue is that she'll start off thinking I'm spontaneous. That I'm comfortable in making unprompted, impulsive decisions. Really, the rule is I'm uncomfortable." He wipes his forehead. "And over time she'd come to realize this. What do I say when she realizes who I really am, which is a lover of routine? But not just with the big things, like the time I fall asleep, but the little things . . ."

"Like?"

"Like you know. All my shit. The ring stains." Demetri's wooden table was riddled with ring stains. He didn't mind the stains. He never bought coasters. He only made sure that if anyone were to put a cup down that cup would land right over an existing ring stain. Not to protect the wood. "I just like things on top of each other like that," he tells me.

"I know. That's not too bad, Demi."

"Well, they're all like that. These fucking habits."

"Well then you'll be okay."

"Okay well, what do I tell this girl, is what I'm asking

you. Because habits live longer than we do. I mean when we die, we're remembered by them. He always took his toast like that. She always ordered the red." He's pointing and pointing. "We live by them and then are remembered by them . . . so that all we are when we die is really just a collection of decisions we made so often that we stopped making them. That's my point. We are remembered by a series of decisions we made so often that we stopped making them. We like to be efficient. To eliminate choice for ourselves—let's replace real desire let's replace our free will."

"Right."

"But then at the end of your fucking life you're wondering what in the fuck did I actually even do, or feel, for myself. Unless you're an artist." He looks at me like he's caught me in something. Suddenly everything on him and in him—every bone—is very still. "If you are an artist you get to escape this whole thing. If you're an artist you're remembered for your work. You transcend your habits. No one really knows Sappho's *habits*. No one knows Shakespeare's habits. Their habits are irrelevant. Though the truth is I felt much closer to Hemingway once I knew his habits. And that he wrote standing up and all that. But I think ultimately, I respect the person who *has* no habits. A person who lives most freely. But then, of course, living freely becomes a habit and loses its charm. So what do I say? Do I tell her this? Maybe she'll think I'm condescending. Because she knows this already. Because we all know this already."

"We do," I say. I know he has some kind of point but I've lost it. I'm only following his energy.

"And then one day"—he's no longer talking to me—"I'll have to make some huge fucking admission. I'd have to give her source material for my personality. Something complex enough to keep feeding into her sense of my potential for depth. And then what if it doesn't work."

"Demetri."

"Because that's a great fear, I think, Ava, that we tell someone everything about ourselves and they say, 'You know, you don't go down as deep as I thought. I can see the bottom of you.' "

"Demetri."

"I don't even know what I'd say. To tell her anything that has actually happened would be like seeking congratulations. But then if I *don't* tell her I'll just be congratulating myself on my own restraint." He's rubbing hard at his temples. "Or I *do* tell her—something totally strange, like I let my mother walk into the sea and drown . . ." I look down. "And this girl's going to think I can think nothing complicated in the present moment because everything complicated is behind me. Because that's the plot of my life. And that's grotesque. But also maybe true."

I say nothing. Demetri knows that I won't. My mind

cleaves white. Until—with a clarity that surprises me—I think of our mother walking up the steep hill to our house. She had one friend in our town, named Audrey, who she liked to go on walks with. Audrey dressed like our mother and said things to Demetri and me like "I'm speaking with my mouth" every time she spoke to us. She thought this was hilarious. Audrey and our mother told each other things: They were going to go out auditioning together. My mother would move beyond the commercials our father wrote for her. They'd take trips to the city and branch out. They'd start a production company themselves. They'd only hire each other. I knew Audrey would never. She had an underactive imagination that liked to be taken over. Our mother was then growing quickly and increasingly deluded and ready to subsume. Sometimes Audrey couldn't keep up. Sometimes they let Demetri walk with them. "What do they talk about?" I asked him once. "Audrey doesn't talk," was all he said.

At Awang, my mother's face pounds into my consciousness, and I haven't spoken. The woman I pointed to earlier is picking up her order. She has a beautiful speaking voice. I gather my focus. "Who is it?" I ask. "I mean tell me the real thing. Who is the woman? Who are you talking about? You don't want me to meet her?"

"You know." But he doesn't say her name.

"The Italian," I say. He only nods. "Okay. And the issue?"

He sighs. "She's in America. But she hasn't contacted me, and I don't know if I should get ahold of her."

I ask him why not.

"We met the last time she was here. Just two months ago." When he leans forward, he rubs his hands over his eyes. The people seated at the table beside us look at him. His feet tap the back legs of my chair. "Soon after we got back from Italy. She was here in the city the day of that *Chronos* opening. It's why I didn't go. I was with her."

"I thought you were ill."

"I was ill," he says. "Because I knew she was here, in town."

I push my pot away.

"You don't even go to your openings." Demetri springs forward. "You don't even know who shows up."

"Yes, but I like when you go."

"But I wasn't going to invite her to your thing. And then what if I went on my own and saw her there. And then if she fell in love with me, it'd be through you."

I protest. "That does not tend to happen."

"It does." Again his feet tapping the back of my chair. "I'm there at your show and I watch women think maybe they're falling in love with me, when really it's with your work and I just happen to be there and catch the excess. Or they don't love the work. Equally possible. But then they want to feel the things they think they *should* be feeling.

So I'm there. They give me the imitation of a feeling. Or, I don't know, the periphery of a feeling. I don't know."

I put a napkin under my coke can. "Or, Demetri, what you think of as peripheral is actually center."

"Oh boy." He leans back.

"That's the point of my work, maybe: to take all the weight of all your suppressed peripheral sensations, over your whole life long, seriously, and in my art I center them, glorify them and give them focus, so that the totality—"

"We're not talking about your work." Demetri laughs.

"I know. I'm talking about you."

"As if I'm part of your work."

"You are."

He looks at his plate.*

"So most interest in me must be facilitated—awakened—through what you do . . ." Demetri thinks. A mushroom bows over his chopsticks. "Never mind," he says.

I am not in a position to tell Demetri that Nati had emailed me that morning. In fact, I had only then officially learned her name, from her caps lock signature. Her email to me was cold but eager: *We met a couple months ago. In my city, by chance. Although not formally. You only stood there, outside, a hard stance with that tilt in your hips.* I

**Plate*, watercolor on rice paper, small
Think of someone you know well and have been to dinner with. Think of the way they look at a plate when it arrives before them. It's the energy with which they look that is in this.

did not breathe but kept reading. She was reinventing her Rome gallery, which she named Minni. They hoped to fill the entranceway with a few large, permanent pieces, and asked if I might contribute. *You'd really be giving us a piece as a gift, essentially*, she wrote. *We would try never to have to sell it . . .*

. . . You only stood there, outside, a hard stance with that tilt in your hips. In front of Demetri, I try to decide why exactly I am withholding this.

"But so, you two met," I say, "when she was last here."

"Yes. Just, maybe, a month or so ago. It was all kind of rushed and coincidental. She called me right when I was out. She happened to be staying nearby. She came with me to the grocery store. To Morton's. She was on her way somewhere. Some kind of event. She'd forgotten to pick up food." I watch him shovel rice down his throat.

"And?"

"And nothing."

"And what? How did she make you feel?"

Demi looks like it is all too much and also like he is dying to tell me.

"Demetri, she makes you feel what? Different? That you have to have her tastes? Italians are persuasive that way."

Demetri leans back now. "I can't explain it to you. No. She forced me in literally fifteen minutes to have tastes. But about things I never would have considered. I mean at the supermarket for example she picks up an orange and asks which half I like, because one half is, I think, the *pediculo*"—he holds out his hand—"and the other half is the *restos del estilo*." His bad Italian accent. "But more than that. I can't say." He pushes his hair back. "She writes off anyone she suspects might not be bursting with life."

"Are you bursting with life?"

"She's very methodical." Demetri sits up in his chair. He laces his fingers together. "I mean in the way she tries to get to know people. Like she'll ask a question all sphinxy like she knows it's so ridiculous to be asking, and then there's this laugh like she spends her whole life laughing, testing to see whether you'll be laughing." Demetri looks at me, desperate. "I mean, she could ask me my favorite color and I would take twenty minutes to respond, because what if she used it against me. I mean she makes me feel a little threatened. It's nice. But this is only after a meeting. In the supermarket. I don't know."

I tell him Nati must have found it all very charming. He shakes his head—his zigzag* part coming through like a muscle.

"Well, she's here, I mean she's back in America. And she hasn't said a word." Here, he turns, so he can stretch his legs and cross his ankles. He seems now to address another version of himself. "What's really the case is that I thought

---

**Zigzag*, acrylic on unprimed cotton canvas, large
You will see an egg-white strip of scalp. It will look spongy and you'll want to finger it.

we laughed very hard together. I'm sure that we did. I remember at one point, in front of the peanut butter, she even got on the floor. I think because of all the varieties. She couldn't believe it. 'Chunky,' she kept saying. 'Extra chunky. Smooth.' She read out all the brand names. And then, I mean, she bent down laughing, just saying the word "chunky," repeating the words "extra chunky." I remember because she folded at the hips as she laughed, and I thought of taking her." I picture what must've been the distance between his eyes and her body. "And if you ask me about what, I mean, if you ask me what *exactly* was funny, what *really* set her off, I can't remember. Which feels miserable." He looks up, then back at me. "I feel stupid. Maybe she didn't laugh that hard. I don't know." I expect him to stop. "There are genres of stupidity, you know—there's the stupidity of simply not knowing things. And then there's the stupidity of not remembering what you once knew. In both cases, the knowledge is not there. But the second one . . . the forgetting . . . you wonder how deep it goes: What else do I not even know that I no longer know? How much of myself am I losing and have I already lost? What will be left of me?"

"Oh my god."

"Ava." He sighs, but he's laughing. "I know. It's horrible. You need to understand an entirely new space is being carved out in my brain and I am in pain."

I think of my own hollow feeling, which is present any

time I know something that Demetri doesn't—I begin to try to tell him that, in fact, she has contacted me. I am interrupted.

"Excuse me?" It's a woman's voice. She's standing beside me, her waist is at my shoulder. I look up to find crisp green eyes. Light, fluttering lids.

"Hi," I say.

She says she works in the area. She's the publicist of a man Demi and I know. She'd been to a few openings and recognizes me. Her cheeks grow red. She says kind things to me and about my work.

"Thank you. And actually, this is my brother, Demetri." I watch her look at him and pick up on all that's overknown to me. Demetri is too polite not to smile and nod, but he does not look at her. You're missing the eyes, I want to tell her, thinking he might still look up.

The woman smiles gently. "So nice to meet you," she says. She stands there for a minute. Orders continue around us. Someone wants a new fork and an extra napkin. At last the woman walks away. Demetri is silent.

"Will you tell me if you end up meeting with her?" I ask. "I mean Nati."

"I won't have a choice," he says. "I'll tell everyone."

I remind him that the whole conversation started with me. About how I need to find someone to fall in love with.

"Just do what you can," he says. He pushes his chair back. I stand up first.

I'M THINKING NOW of Nati's bedroom. All the lights. Fairy lights tacked to the walls. Novelty lamps made of wrapped copper. Porcelain lamps shaped like bloated amoebae. Glass lamps blown taut into spheres. I'm thinking of the time she sat cross-legged on her carpeted bedroom floor, cutting her toenails. "It is good that Demetri sees lots of things, but not into things," she said to me.

"Why is that good?" I was standing, watching.

"Because," she said from underneath her hair, "because I read about it. That once you really see *into* things, once you understand everything, you know nothing can be done. You become a sociopath. You become psycho, crazy, because you know there's nothing you can do." The sound of her clipping. "I read that once."

TWO WEEKS AFTER we meet at Awang, Demetri and I find Nati at an anniversary party. The party's in a big, box-like apartment. When you enter, all you see is a kitchen to the left and a wide-open space to the right with a massive table in the center. Long velvet couches work to divide the space. The couple who lives there—whose anniversary we're celebrating—sleeps in an elevated space right above the kitchen. I can see their unmade bed from where I stand, near the table, talking to James, a music reporter, who is telling me something about the song that's playing and how it was conceived in an Arizona jail by an emaciated petty thief. I'm angled in such a way that Nati cannot see me when she walks in. At hearing her voice, I choke. James keeps talking as I pull chicken from my throat.

"I'm sorry I'm sorry I'm sorry!" Her voice comes from behind me, almost slides up my back. It's my first time seeing her since Rome. When I turn, I notice that she's lost weight and a bit of her tan. Her hair has blackened, her accent thickened. I watch as she bends to slip off her waxed-cotton coat and unclip her braided hair, the smell of sweet mint unraveling. "I'm so sorry, I got caught!" She addresses someone I don't know. "Hi, hi!"

James is still beside me. I am slouching, and in front of him I try to fix myself into a smile as Nati continues through the foyer and into the kitchen. She kisses everyone, tilts her head back, and motions toward alcohol. "Yes!" someone says. Through chatter I hear the smack of glass on granite and then catch wine being poured, thin red and bright. "Cows' blood," Nati says, smiling into it. She keeps speaking, but as she turns her voice is overlapped. Too many people in a room. The anniversary we're celebrating marks twenty years of coupledom between Tom, a baker, and Paul, an architect famous for his high-profile zoning analyses. (A week earlier, drunk at a bar, Paul described Nati to another friend of ours: "She's pretty layered," he said. It was from him—and not Demetri—that I learned how often Nati traveled from Europe to America, how often she organized shows at her gallery in Rome—which was where she wanted my piece—how she sprung up out of nowhere, her furious work ethic, how he thought she was not necessarily beautiful, but very *aesthetic*.)

I try to look past James to find Demetri. My eyes circle the room, speeding through faces . . . twenty not-Demetris until—neck, collar, shoulder—his back to the party. I consider going to him, preparing him. But he is with Paul—the more severe half of the couple—whose long body tilts forward, making it clear he is angling for a chat, but only with my brother, whose knowledge he enjoys exploiting. At parties Demetri functions as a big globe people like to wrap around, hoping to impress themselves and one another with intellectual latitude. Tonight I catch comments on the legal legacy of the Korean War, on the molecular structure of certain South American peppers, on why Demetri likes the taste of mold. Just before Nati arrived I stood listening for when his laughter—a sequence of high-pitched honks—interrupted the conversations around him. He'd been honking right when Nati came in. She has not heard him and does not know he's in the room.

I cannot go and get him, I remind myself. I focus again on James. "What?" I keep asking him. It's hard to hear. I realize then that his smile, its condescension, is to tell me it is too early to be spilling on myself. "Ave, you zoning," he says. I look down at my new stain.

On my right side, Nati stands in the kitchen and pours herself another glass, just as Tom lowers the music and announces dinner.

"Hiiii!" He rings a bell. "Can all please be seated! Where's baby Paul?"

Paul turns from Demetri—I see he wears an *Only Sausage in My Oven* apron despite not doing any cooking, and despite being a vegetarian, and despite publicly claiming to hate having sex with Tom, and men in general. He sighs and makes his way toward Tom, annoyed that this dinner will actually have to include a dinner. Everyone else heads for the long table. I watch Demetri check his watch and then look up. He sees me, waves, sees Nati, stands still, reddens.* I feel the guilt unique to that which cannot be controlled.

Everyone sits down. Demetri and I are placed at a diagonal from Nati—he is still red, getting redder. I have the urge to put my feet on his face and stomp. But attention is soon refocused—people grow quiet as Paul and Tom speak near the stove.

"No," Tom is saying, "I want the custard just set."

"Yes, I know." Paul takes a sip of something.

"Okay."

"Okay?"

**Reddens*, oil on linen, medium
Why do paintings of a single color take me the longest?

Demetri kicks me under the table. I look at him but he does not look at me, and I realize he thought I was a table leg.

"I mean," Tom goes on, "I want it just set, but to still be hot—like hot with a little wiggle in the middle."

"You guys talk about my body like you're eating it." It's Nati, who presses her hands into her stomach.

"Stop, Nati, you look amazing."

"Stop!"

"No, like you literally look so young."

"You literally look fucking fetal."

Nati, who looks thirty at age thirty-one, laughs. "I do feel a little, um, unhatched."

Demetri laughs but keeps his eyes down, as Nati, as if seeing him for the first time, beams in his direction. *You*, is what she wants to seem to be thinking. She has yet to look right at me.

"There." It's Paul behind me. I don't turn toward him, but I listen as he and Tom consider which tins to use for dessert. Paul wants to use the muffin tins.

"I don't want a deep tart," Tom says. "Saucer tins, for shallow tarts."

"Okay," Nati says from the table. She's speaking over others, but with a nonaggressive superiority. "I want a shallow tart."

"Nati wants a warm, shallow tart," Paul says.

"Deep in my mouth," Nati says, laughing.

"We're gonna give it to you."

Oil pools in my stomach as dinner is served. Savory pies: lattice crusts break through to soft chunks of white-pink ham, wilted peas, layers of bottom pastry rubberized by juices. Someone is talking about renovating their kitchen. Someone else about the limits of irony. Demetri is silent but not frowning. The man next to Nati is explaining how he can no longer sit outside.

"Mmm, yes. It's because of the chickaddas?" Nati asks with her mouth open and full. Then she closes it, puts her hand over her mouth, but continues to speak. "Sorry. The chickaddas? Right?" No one can figure her out. She mimes fear at her own incoherence. "Wait. What is it? No?! Chickaddas!"

Demetri: "You mean cicadas, the insect, like *sick-aida*. That's how we say it."

Nati's eyes widen. She grabs the shoulder of the man next to her and puts her palm over her face. "Yes!" She slams the man, almost collapses into him—he looks bewildered and warmed by her attention. But she is staring only at my brother. She looks at him as she enunciates: "Sick-aida."

Demetri nods. "The bug."

She nods. "The bug." In the last beat, though, she looks at me.

I take a sip of water. This is it. I realize I've been waiting for it: Nati is going to ask me, in front of everyone, why I never answered her queries about the gallery. She'll be charming: *And Ava, busy lady, I've contacted you three times. You're too good for me?* She'll laugh. I prepare myself with any excuse I can say out loud, and then realize I have none.

But Nati looks away. And soon some obscure saint diverts my attention with a question on some new work—my *Falling in Love* series, and then the *Getting Someone to Fall in Love with Me* series. I feel Nati overhearing my answers, so I don't bother correcting the titles and say yes, and then yes to more pepper, more wine. The talk continues. At school, Moche's seven-year-old is accidentally drawing swastikas and Demetri is consulted as to whether or not this is okay. He thinks about it, explains with practiced objectivity that there is a decision to make between teaching the child symbolism or encouraging formalism, which is to say between encouraging ideas or pure aesthetics, and that he'd probably choose the latter even if it makes him a bad Jew. I can feel his words glancing off Nati, who sits watching Demi's right hand as he lifts and drops his napkin.*

More conversations break out and the volume increases. Demetri and I are the only two who are sweating. I stop speaking halfway through my sentence to join Nati in

---

**Napkin*, oil on linen, medium
The napkin Demetri was lifting and putting down had some lipstick on it for reasons still unknown to me.

listening to Vanessa—who is saying she switched to women at age twenty-three, something about all men being fake cunts and wanting real cunt; Vanessa and her wife smile at each other with unbelievable affection. Next to them Peter announces that his father is just dying dying dying, but it isn't so bad as all that, which Nati says is very reassuring.

Demetri does not eat his food. Neither do I. We sit and wait for more of her. "No," I at last hear Nati say. She is sipping from her third glass of red, her square jaw cutting into the round rim. Demetri listens beside me. "My grandfather was a farmer," Nati says. Someone farther down the table is speaking to her. She almost has to yell: "We were! Very poor. Yes. No, I'm glad you know. Heaven forbid I come across as not having suffered. I swear I am not nearly as spoiled as I look. Although they always told me I was spoiled. It's because I liked the scalloped trim on my dresses. You're so spoiled, Natalia, with your scalloped trim. *Sei viziata*. But you know, I said to them, You misunderstand me! You think *this* is spoiled? You can't even *imagine* how spoiled I could be! If really given the chance. You think this is desire? This is wanting something? You have no idea. Anyway, no one listened to me. I had asthma and was coughing all the time. I was this little coughing . . . idiot . . . who needed a scalloped trim. No one laughed at me. No one had a good sense of humor. They were too busy, martyrdom is busywork."

Tom stands to collect the plates: "I'm so glad we know,

Nati. Though we wouldn't be mad if you hadn't. I mean if you hadn't suffered. We wouldn't hold it against you."

Paul stands to help. "Well, we wouldn't hold it against you in *front* of you. Or *before* you."

Nati lifts her hands. "Prepositions!" *Prep-o-ze-shonz*. Earlier, Nati had been discussing the classes she was taking to improve her English, how prepositions confused her ("I am never sure of them, or about them").

Tom clicks his tongue. He laughs as he lifts my plate. "What else? We wouldn't hold it against you along you? About you? Behind you?"

"I'll hold it against you"—it's Demetri—"on top of you."

Nati draws a breath. Demetri looks down. I put down my fork. A beat passes before Nati leans back and loses herself laughing.

"Demetri!" Tom says. "What a pig." He taps Demetri's shoulder.

Nati sighs and sets her gaze deep on Demetri and says, "Not *pig*. Bug." Her nose flares and she smiles. A big one, where the gaps between her teeth fill with light, as if they are not gaps but little portals into the pit of her throat. Demetri grows nervous beside me. He stiffens. I think he might break out into laughter or choke, but someone cuts in with a question. Something about distribution rights. In an effort to stay focused Demetri asks two thousand questions to clarify the question before he gives an answer. At the same time, the only child in the room (eight years old, graphite eyes, bobbed brown hair) asks Nati to braid her hair. "I actually don't know how," Nati laughs. "I'm sorry. My neighbor did this for me," she says. "And since he likes to do it he's never taught me. Control . . ." and then I can't hear the rest.

At last everyone stands. Time for dessert. There would be lots of shallow tarts up on the roof. The joke, like the other jokes, was made for Nati, who smiles, but who stays half-seated as the others rise—I hear her low behind me, saying "Hi"—she's so close I think at first she's talking to me, and in that moment I think everything has fallen into place, and that she has meant it to be for me, and that I will have to quietly react. That we have some kind of alliance. But she's talking to Tom. She wishes she could stay, but she has to leave early to meet a friend—"So I'm just going to slip out," she hums.

Tom sighs as he hand dries and stacks the plates. Nati whispers something else in his ear, as her job is to casually dispense secrets, and kisses him. Tom's cheeks are singed with alcohol and oven heat, and I imagine her lips cool him.

As she finds her jacket Tom collects more plates. He repeats the word *ciao* and Nati smiles. She doesn't turn around again as she walks out the door, and Demetri, hidden by me, Vanessa, and Paul, is unable to watch her go.

I RUN INTO NATI shortly after the party. Bad timing. Because in the following days Demetri and I do not discuss her. We don't do a postmortem. Demetri doesn't ask me what I think of her, of the things she said or how she moved around a room. He does not wonder if I think she looked at him for sustained periods of time. If I think the jokes between them landed with them alone, or if their subtle undercurrent of conversation—if there was one—was perceptible, if it made any others feel a certain way.

I don't tell him that by the end of the night I think she looked at me more than she looked at him. That to me, when she joked with him it was to prove to me her ease and humor. How my egotism convinces me that every word she spoke was spoken so that I could sit there and analyze it. Plus, she wants my art, Demetri, which is the greatest form of wanting me. But I say nothing.

And then, when I am the one who runs into her, a week later, autumn in full bloom, I stop short. There is a small café with slim chairs for outdoor seating. It's near my apartment, on a block dense with brownstones and overrun by strollers. I should have known her by her back, draped in a light white shawl. But I refuse to see it. When I walk by her, she calls out my name.

"Hi!"

"Hi!"

"I didn't know you were still in town," I say.

She's holding a plastic cup full of iced tea, and gestures to the empty chair. I tell her I am in a hurry. Quickly, I calculate the probability of Demetri finding us. He does not live far away. "It's not broken," Nati says of the chair, which has a violent crack down its center.

I tell her again I can't stop for too long. I do not tell her that one reason, small but insistent, is because I know right away I'd be degrading her beauty, its stately imprecision. Her hair is up. Her broad cheeks are two cool, dry planes. I try not to look. Her eyes are uneven, looking mildly in two directions. They are glass-black. I watch as they reflect the tumble of leaf light, which comes through each pupil in an orange quiver that I briefly mistake for her pulse. Demetri would not breathe, I think.

"I'm here at least for the next couple months, actually," Nati says, taking pleasure, I imagine, in pronouncing all four syllables of *act-ju-all-eee*, and remaining oblivious to my being oblivious to everything but her neck, her small ears.

"Very nice," I say. I think of the polite things: "So are you enjoying your stay? Fall is beautiful."

"It is." Nati looks around in confirmation.

We're interrupted when two children pass by, one on a scooter, one on foot. Both screeching. They are followed by a thin, tall woman. She's striking. Her face, like Nati's, is large and structural. But her eyes are too small, her nose a jagged rock. She's so tall that I imagine if Demetri were here she'd tower over him.

"I wish I were so tall." Nati follows the woman with her eyes, which squint at different degrees, wrinkles piling higher on her right. "Is it strange that I feel if I were taller my thoughts would be better? More open, more room to grow. I'm not even being funny about it."

"I think that, too," I say.

Nati nods, waiting for more from me, which without Demetri people tend to do.

"I want to be tall," I continue. "It'd be nice for people to look at me and think that I'm thinking and feeling the best and most interesting thing available to think and feel in that moment."

"Are you?"

"Thinking the most interesting thing? No," I say. "Never. I'm never the one. I'm always waiting for the other person to think it, then to say it."

"That's pressure." She's smiling.

"You'll come up with something."

We're silent. "I'd like to see that woman again," I say. Nati looks at me and nods. She's about to speak, but I go on. "I mean I want to be alone with her. I have this feeling, sometimes, like I don't want anyone else to be able to see a very beautiful thing until I've figured it out, until I've understood the strength behind it."

"You want to keep her?" Nati opens her purse.

"Yes," I say. "I'm extremely territorial over beauty that is not mine. Everyone who has it—I want to keep them in my house." I keep talking as she searches. "Just to watch them, figure out their mechanics."

"I don't know if it's a strength, Ava." She enunciates both *A*s in my name. "Beauty, I mean. Is not a strength. Just an accident."

"But many strengths are accidental," I say. "Like height." I can see down into her purse. The pattern on the inseam is a beige crosshatch. I watch her open a zippered compartment and pull out a straw.

"And then weakness?" she asks. She puts one end of the straw in her mouth, the other in her tea, and starts sucking.

"I don't know anything about weaknesses. I have too many. I'm too attuned to them to understand them very well." I'm only talking so she can finish her sip.

"You're not," she says, and sucks again.

"Not what?"

"Attuned to them." There is such attention in her look. I sense a joke that I can't place. I have to match it. She knows this. I don't blink. She goes on: "No one who feels strongly about their weaknesses really believes they have them."

I don't answer. Nati laughs again and I notice a pale slit on her bottom lip where the lipstick has not touched. I resist the urge to run my thumb along her mouth.

I don't mention that Demetri would roll his eyes at this exchange. He could not bring himself to believe in the absurdity that beauty played any role in conceptions of strength, or weakness. And that despite Harvard and history he forgot how from the beginning of time certain children have been chosen over others because of the anticipated shape of a jaw. Any kind of immense interweaving of history and morality and beauty, I remind myself, or convince myself, is lost on him.

I look at her tea, which she's placed on her notebook so that her pages won't lift in wind. I am going to ask her what she is working on when I notice, to the right of her notebook, a pen with a triangle tip—a pre-filled fountain pen, whose blue barrel bears the manufacturer's logo E.M.

My brother uses that pen, I am going to tell her. At the thought of his name I feel him behind me and turn around. Or rather I start to turn around, before I realize that if he is there—which I know he is not—I do not want to see him just yet. From Nati's perspective I am still only staring at her table. On my way to meet her eyes I catch my own reflection in the café window, and I revolt. Nati laughs.

"The same thing happened to me!" she says. "That's why I'm facing this way, to make sure I'm not just staring at myself."

"But why wouldn't you?" I ask.

"Why wouldn't I what?" Her eyes soften.

"Never mind. They put too much metal in there."

Nati taps the window. "You mean in this glass?"

"Yes," I say, arching over her and tapping it myself. "Metal is why it's reflective."

"You don't like to see your face?" Something in the way she asks me this, her mouth lifts but not into a smile.

"No," I say. I like being immediate with her.

"Not even your eyes?"

"Oh god . . . is there more of me?"

"But your eyes, Ava. You know what they write about you? I mean about your eyes."

"No."

"That you look at people and you make them feel dead." Now she is full-on smiling. "I mean you make them feel dead inside. It's the intensity. Destroys people. That's just what they say." She is flattering me.

"Am I making you feel dead inside?"

"No. They say you only do it to people you like. Or respect. But I feel very alive when you look at me, so now I know you must hold a grudge." She's still smiling.

My toes shut down.

"You know," I say, pointing to her straw. "They're trying to outlaw those."

"I know." She takes a sip. "That's why one must always be sure to carry them." She bites her straw and shows me all her teeth. Red sun rides up her face, stopping at her lashes, spreading her open. The next wind puts her hair over her face, and then whips it back.

I look again at her outfit: a symphony in white, starting in eggshell earrings and ending in smoke with her shoes. I think of her closet. It must be a walk-in, and circular. It must have mirrors everywhere. The clothes must be coordinated by color. Maybe by texture, too. She must make her way around, her fingers pressing into winter furs, sliding over silks, catching in spaghetti straps. Her breath as she stands before every item, watching it hang limp without her body, that sigh when you're alone with your own gross abundance.

"Well, enjoy your time here," I say.

"Right, right. You're running."

"Walking really, really fast."

"Elbows!" She mimes the motion.

I begin moving away, half-backward. "I hope you grow," I say. I raise my arm high as if to shout, TALLER!

"I will!" She says it with the air of not quite having heard me. But she crosses her fingers above her head.

I feel her watch me walk away. In fact, I've turned in the wrong direction, so that I am going back the way I came. I am thinking only of the image of Demetri's handwriting, his blue ink in a journal, his standing in the drugstore just last week, sifting through packets of pens, weighing various packs on his palm, convinced* some chambers held

---

**Convinced*, acrylic on ceramic plate
Another plate because I ran out of material. How to explain the colors in this?

more ink than others. "*That's* how they get you," he said to me.

"They don't," I said.

"Oh yes," he said. "They get you."

IN THE COMING WEEKS, Demetri does not know I begin to dream about her. And that in those dreams Nati is touching me and looking at me like the very act of existence is the strangest thing and thank god she is touching me and looking at me. He doesn't know that I sketch my memory of her in my notebooks, or that I would like to know how often she flosses, the way she sleeps. The kinds of things she thinks when placed on hold. But that's okay. Because at this point I've yet to ask myself a central question—which is whether my feelings toward Nati are the result of my trying to outpace Demetri's desire, or if my desire for Nati is entirely my own. I'm embarrassed to say that this question had not occurred to me yet. Not with the necessary clarity. Only as a thrumming unease, relegated to the very back of the back brain.

I think of telling Demetri that Nati has requested work from me, for a contribution to Minni, or that after meeting her outside the café I finally answered her email and asked

---

Convinced (cont.): It's the color of the way you feel when someone seems convinced of something that you know to be false.

her to give me a topic. He does not know that she has not answered this email, that it's been three weeks, and that her silence has been consuming me.

And this is why, when Demetri at last calls me (he had been unusually quiet), saying, "Nati got in touch with me," it feels like revenge. I remind myself he knows nothing. "She literally just got in touch with me," he tells me, his voice exuberant. "Strange timing." Quickly, the purity of his joy diminishes my pain. I sense him pacing as he speaks. "She called me. She wants my thoughts on the history of architecture in New York. I don't know much about it." He's outside so his voice is loud and cut through with wind. "But she remembered my comments on the church, that time. I knew a lot about that demolished church."

"Demetri!" I'm standing in my studio (a large closet with a narrow south-facing window) with a paintbrush in my hand, clenching my ass. I tell him that's amazing. "Why, though?"

"Why what?"

"Why the church? That topic?" Though I thought I remembered.

"She's bringing a gallery here. They'll be occupying the first floor of a certain building. And they want to honor it or something. Discuss its history at the opening. She just wants to kind of consult with me first, I guess. Anyway." He asks if she told me.

"I can't remember. No."

"Oh."

"When would she have told me?" I ask.

"I don't know. At the party, maybe. Tom and Paul's. She kind of looked like she had something she wanted to tell you."

"Oh," I say.

"Oh," Demetri says. I can tell there's more. "Because she mentioned to me, when everyone was talking, something about wanting work for the Rome gallery, for Minni. I didn't know if she had asked you or . . . maybe she wanted me to ask you . . ."

I go mildly blank. "Oh yeah."

"Oh yeah what?"

"I have to give them something. I forgot."

"So then she did ask you," he says.

"Yes."

"What will you give them?"

"I haven't thought about it. But Demetri, that's amazing."

I hear him start to smile to himself. "Well, she wants to meet me soon, to talk about the new space, I think."

"And clearly she wants to know more about you, Demi. Amazing."

"Amazing," he says.

"I just mean that this means you two are talking."

"For now. Why?"

"Because that's good for you." I can't tell if he knows he's being difficult.

"It is. Good—" He's panting into the phone. I imagine him rushing to cross a street, his free hand held up to stop* an onslaught of taxis and Toyotas. "So you two aren't talking then?"

"No."

"Okay." We wait. His heavy breathing covers his mood, or any hints of suspicion or relief. "I have a job, by the way," he tells me. "I'm finally on board. Another company."

"What do you mean on board?" I ask. My mind is still blank but I am operating, and I remind myself that Demetri, since being fired, insisted he was going to take another job only if it was an actual advancement.

"On board? Like I'm finally on staff."

"What company?"

"A firm, like a speaking firm," he says.

"You're giving speeches?"

"Hi." He's talking to a dog. "Sorry. No. I do research for people who have to give speeches. It's called Big Talk. I'm in the Future and Storytelling division."

"You have to research what they tell you?"

"Yes . . . that's the point."

"I see."

"I'm glad you see."

**Stop*, oil on linen, medium
One color—all fattened up—halts another.

I don't answer. I hear the chime of his entry somewhere. "Ava, this is a very good thing."

"I know," I say, resuming my painting. I'm working on a series of photorealistic, life-size shampoo bottles. Next to each bottle I plan to paint a woman whose body shape mirrors that of the bottle. At the time I'm not sure what I'm going for. I'm hoping it will be more than recreational art, which is to say more than just a comment on the increasing biomorphism of our plastics, or the inverse (the increasing plasticity of our bodies). "I thought maybe you'd think it was another piano," I say to Demetri. "I mean not quite what you want to do."

"That doesn't matter," he says.

"Well, but you convinced me that it did," I say, attending to my bottle, using silver to thin out the intensity of my green, trying to get that plastic translucence.

"It's less piano. It's out of film completely, and so less tangentially related to what I want."

"It's really not related at all."

"Which is good," he says. "Do you not just say congratulations?"

"I did say congratulations."

"No," Demetri says. "Only the tone of your voice is congratulatory. It will be money for me."

"And that's amazing."

"Ava, thanks. Can you please say something real."

"I did!"

"Okay, go again."

"Okay." I put my brush down, as if this will help me keep my voice light. I tell him I'm confused about why he's signing on to something that will limit his freedom, however mildly. "And it's terrible to say out loud but I actually do want you to succeed, you know, in feeling free."

"Good, go on," he says. The wind through his end is gone. He's inside the supermarket. I can hear the soft pop. I imagine him surrounded by canned tuna and jars of berry preserves.

"That's it," I say.

"I need this job. Being beholden to you is a limit to my freedom."

"Beholden!" I step away from the canvas. The only items I'd bought for him recently were a bag of discount peaches and an old Tom Waits CD that was incompatible with his computer. That morning, I'd sent a check to his landlord to cover his next month's rent, though he did not know this yet, and would never bring it up.

"Ava, congratulate me."

"You never congratulate me!" I find myself saying.

"Ava, I don't congratulate you because you're always congratulating yourself. Everyone congratulates you."

"Because you don't."

"Why do you need my congratulations?"

I tell him I don't *need* them.

"So then what the fuck, Ava."

"Well do you need mine?" I know his answer.

"No, never mind."

We wait.

"Demetri."

"What?" When I don't answer, he only sighs. "Okay," he says. I hear noise on his end. The sound of a cash register. "Thank you."

NATI'S NEW YORK GALLERY OPENS. There's a party. I don't go. I'm not surprised Nati did not email me an invitation, as we are engaged in that modern phenomenon of sustaining two conversations at once: one online, where we are formal and distant (*Dear Nati*, *Dear Ava*), and one in person, where we are a bit warmer, competitive. I imagine the party. The music. I figure at this point in the night she and Demetri have spoken. I imagine Demetri's hands at a social event—the way he spreads out his fingers when he's trying to think of something to say. The way he tilts forward at a joke he's working up to tell.

I imagine the gallery is crowded and they're chatting and she's forced up against him. And her hair smells like it's still wet and her lashes carry the curve of light. I imagine she feels his body brittle* with height and very warm.

****Brittle***, pencil, crayon, and synthetic polymer paint on paper, large
The amount of paper and crayon on this actually made the paper brittle, with the same worn softness of a child's drawing that contains the entire box of Crayola.

I imagine Demetri saying my name. And he says it like they both know something about me. That this makes them embarrassed, but sharing the knowledge is a kind of refuge.

In the meantime, that night, I try to research a permanent home for my work—a gallery to support me. I read more reviews of my recent art. I shuffle through tepid praise, middling stances, dismissals. The dismissals are mostly because I've listened to Demetri and have gone more abstract. I'd recently tried to distill colors from medieval icons and turn the result into something modern—beyond the broad, layered strokes of the moderns before me. But at the release of this work (Why describe failure? Just imagine that I used a microscopic, pencil-tip paintbrush when a large fan brush was required, and I did this over and over again)—at the release of this work the few who wrote about me claimed that I was still merely replicating. One article used me as a small example of "our larger cultural malaise." Our inability to create the new. If there was ever proof art was at its end, I carried a bit of its death inside me. The horror of this made me laugh. Demetri's line is busy when, the morning after the opening, I try him.

I WAIT FOR HIM to call so he can tell me everything, and so we can assess.

Nothing. Two weeks pass.

Instead, Nati sends me a message. I read her words with her voice in my head, and it makes me arch upward. She at last wants to talk about the piece I'm to paint for Minni. *We can have a phone chat about it, whatever you prefer.* In my anxiety, I write to her: *Come over, soon, to discuss.*

She does. She enters my apartment purse-first: it's heavy with a binder. She explains that she's going to need information from me. That I'm going to have to fill out paperwork to do with rights and ownership and whatnot. As she speaks, I watch her hair. She has cut it. It is black and short and suspends a half inch over her shoulders. She's curled the ends, and now everything on her curves at that same degree, the skin over her cheekbones, her nose, the ridge of her brow—all the arcs drive her face forward. But she herself is reserved—very formal. I wonder if she understands my energy and wants to avoid it, if she hopes she can redirect it into paper, the checking of boxes and signing of forms.

"You have a very strange space, Ava," she says, after laying the binder on my counter. "Which I'm sure flatters you."

I tell her to take off her raincoat. She does, and hands it to me. I hang it up and touch the inseam warm with her back.

"Where is your studio?" she asks me.

I point to the closet.

"Can I see it?"

"No."

Since I know what I'm going to do, I say it quickly: I tell her for her gallery I'm going to paint her. I tell her this will animate her space—having an image of herself there. That she should feel herself radiating from it even when she's not present. No one has to know it's her if she doesn't want them to.

She is silent. She smiles, then stares at me, and then smiles again. "That's what you want?"

I nod. "I think that it would be best," I say.

"Ava." She looks at me soft, though she stands straight. "I'm sorry, but I think you misunderstand me."

"How?" We pause. I tell her to sit down. "Never mind," I say. I offer her coffee. "We won't make you look that vulnerable." I am curious to know if a part of her suspects that I am withholding a question, which is whether, in the meantime, she has fallen a little in love with my brother, and if she plans to have him. She makes no hints either way and never says his name.

"You won't make me look vulnerable? I have a feeling you won't be able to help it. I've seen what you make of people."

"Who told you that?"

"What do you mean?" Her eyes open wide and fasten on me, and I feel trapped and delighted. I realize I'm the one who wants to say his name.

"I mean," I say, but then I can't continue. "We can do

whatever you want." I tell her I could destroy her face if she wants. "I could dissemble it. Put your nose here." I point at her chin—my finger so close to her skin. "And your mouth there, upside down. Your neck parted down the middle. Your eyes rolling across the canvas."

"That would be a trip."

"The problem," I say, handing her a mug, "is that I'm not particularly good with fabrics."

She says nothing. She only puts the cup to her mouth and blows.

"I mean cottons and wools, those things, it's hard for me to get those right. There's something in the grain I can't bring to life."

"You're better with synthetics?" She takes a sip. "Want to wrap me in plastic? This is silk," she says, pulling at her shirt. "My mother bought it for me."

"It won't do," I say.

She doesn't move.

"Well," I say.

Nati looks at me, and then at the floor. We've agreed to something. I feel a charge up my legs. Then silence. Then she laughs to herself. She starts taking off her clothes. Her neck flexes as her shirt comes over her head. I know she must undress like this always. Yet there's a sense of ceremony—like in taking off her clothes she's getting dressed for something. In the span of three blinks she is braless—immediately bare. I see her all at once: Her breasts light on her chest.

Her bare, lean stomach arches forward as she lifts her hand to move her hair. I notice two darkened, nearly parallel lines at her hips. And then, an inch under her belly button, a long scar down to her pelvis. She sees me staring and points to it: "Girlhood," she says. "Up and off a swing." I want to ask her a question. Anything that might put a pause on our momentum. She folds her silk shirt over a chair; light slicks down the fabric. Then she unzips the back of her skirt. She bends first one leg and then the other to step out of it. The bones in her knees twitch. Muscle runs in a long arc down her calf. The skirt—which was just full with her thighs—is now puddled on the cushion. She stands and is all skin in front of me.

I don't know where to put her. I think of Demetri and suddenly wish it wasn't her at all. But when I think maybe my hands are his, I go in. I feel a sense of power I cannot understand.

"I don't know where to put you, exactly," I say. Her hips feel smaller with my palms on them.

Nati looks around like she'd just been let in. "Hmm," she says. The space between her breasts shows bone. "Can I just stay here?" She gestures just behind her, at the wall.

THE NEXT DAY I wake up and immediately call Demetri. I call him to tell him that Nati was in front of me. That I had put her there. Until he doesn't pick up, and I realize my relief. I want to know nothing about his feeling, but most of all I want to know nothing about my own. I convince myself that one of my many other selves was the one who saw her, and that I myself—my most lived-in, relevant self, my self of that day—had nothing to do with it. I do things to distract myself from her, from any thought of her.

I choose to go to a new grocery store. The aisles confuse me. The items confuse me. I enjoy it. I run my thumb along the metal grooves of an olive jar. Then I go home, and all is as usual. I sketch the shower, I sketch a quarter-used bar of soap. I sketch the soap bubbles themselves, those microscopic rainbow spheres. Then I go outside again, walk around the block. I sketch the sagging fabric of my bodega's red awning. I go to the playground and sketch the green steel machinery: seesaws, concentric steel rings. I sketch the small fountain. Everything, I realize, is gyrational or excreting or frothing. I walk around wiping my palms down my thighs to get her heat off them.

SHE COMES OVER the next night. She's the one who calls me. I paint her twice more. We've agreed that we do this in silence.

"Well," she says out of nowhere, as she's positioned on my floor. "Ava. I have a question."

"If it's fast." I have a brush between my teeth.

She looks up at me. "Never mind."

But she talks anyway. She talks in paragraphs. She knows I am painting her body and that I need her stillness—so she's good at talking with just her mouth, the way a puppeteer uses minute lip gestures to convey an entire personality and interior life. She describes growing up in Italy amid cold kilometers of nothingness. How the mountains in view were pink, and how their pink pigment started to sting her eyes. "Mountains can burn you," she tells me. How eventually geography and nature came to repel her because where she lived they somehow stood in for culture. How everything was static and how nothing ever happened to her. How minutely she remembers all that was said and done to her. (Later she'll contradict herself, she'll tell me that the biggest difference between us is that she knows how to let go of memory, and Demetri and I do not. She'll tell me she can chop off memory like a head. That Italy is an ancient place. That collectively, Italians are so confident in the glory of their past that they never need to think about memory. That this trickles down: "Italians don't psychologize memory and everything," she'll tell me. "But America is still too new," she'll say. "In America you are still collecting yourselves. You are still obsessed with yourselves. All you think about is memory because you're trying to collect more of it and really make it mean something. You're obsessed. And they convince you that it's healthy to be so obsessed, so self-concerned. Demetri and you are obsessed. All Americans are obsessed. Italians are relaxed. I am relaxed." She'll go on in her way. I'll want to refute her. I won't.)

"Will you tell me why you wanted to do this?" she asks me, after a long digression. I panic. I think she means paint her this way, as if it's something I've forced her into. I'm struck by how rapidly I come up with my defenses.

"Wanted to do what?"

"What do you think?"

"Why I wanted to . . ."

"Paint," she says.

"You?"

"No. Generally."

"Oh," I say, sighing and getting on my knees to paint the curve in her back. "Necessity," I say. I tell her—no one had asked me this before and I was testing to see if I was going to mock myself—"If you're born with a totally undeserved and unaccountable feeling of power, you have to make a decision: Will I control others, or will I set others free." I watch the back of her head nod at me. "And so I want to do both," I say. "At all times. And this is the one way for me to do that."

Again we're silent. As I paint, I watch as an energy begins to race around her body. I put down my brush. She's faced away from me but feels me staring.

"Hi," she says.

She comes back the next night for another.

And then the fourth night in a row. I only let her see

half-finished canvases, and only in glances—and I think it's made her hungry.

I'm struggling with my desperation not to know her. She makes it hard. "Tell me something very private about yourself," she says to me. I'm painting her back. I watch her shoulders flex as she points to her own body. "I'll go first," she says, still pointing. "*This*, for example, is not from girlhood." I can tell she's running her finger down the scar under her navel. "Now you."

"What's it from?"

"It's your turn," she says.

"Okay," I say, watching dimples rise along her spine. "I don't wear underwear," I lie for no reason. "I don't like it."

"That's not private."

"I really have nothing private to tell you . . . I'd tell anyone anything," I say. "I have no sense of privacy. No deeply hidden wounds that I can uncover and provide for you." I want to tell her that she should respect me for this. That I know Demetri, against his better judgment, respects me for this.

She only nods, pauses. "Do you know that I stalked you?" she asks. Now she twists her head to face me, her eyes are dark and leveling at me. "When? Eight, nine years ago. I found you in Boston. I was visiting. My friend curated a Cézanne show at the MFA. I went, I saw, got nauseated and then restless. I decided to sit for a coffee near campus. There were these spunky little mugs on the wall.

Attitude in all of them. I asked who it was," she says. I can tell she wants me to look at her. "See? I have an eye. And so, I asked them who it was. I got my hands on that newspaper. The two nudes. And two of Demetri. Nothing about you written. Just your name, and so I asked around. People recognized your brother. I found you where they said you liked to work, and I watched you. In the lobby of that big center. I stood behind you and watched you. I just wanted to see you."

I feel a hot tension in my groin. I can't look at her. She turns to face the wall; I continue painting her back.

"You stood there for how long?"

"A long time. You didn't look up, not once."

I have the urge to look behind me to see if she's still there. The long, lean weight of her watching.

We are silent. I keep painting. Soon, though, she twists around again and this time gets on her knees. She crawls toward me. She stretches up and grabs my hair. I feel my scalp lift off the bone as she pulls. "Thick," is all she says.

I don't think it's going to happen. And it doesn't. She only looks at me, her face hovering right over mine. I feel the wind off her blinks. Then she twists and crawls back to her place. I keep painting. My heart pounding, my eyes feel blind with blood.

Later in the night I have a paintbrush in my hand, the paint at the tip of my brush flesh-colored, and I am in the middle of her, when she peels away from the wall and approaches me. My arm is still bent, and I feel her two fingers dragging me down by my elbow. I put my brush up on the easel on the way to the floor.

I try to begin to say something . . .

"I don't know," she whispers.

When she spreads my legs open, her hair is soft between my thighs. I try to stay still. It's quick breath tightening into nothing into nothing into nothing and then it's all at once: a tight twist at the tip of my brain, and then the coursing through. She digs her nails into my hips. Afterward, she climbs over me and wipes sweat from the back of my neck. She looks quickly at my canvas and then back at me. I see all the angles of her face and understand how much I want her. It feels like a desire that is my own. I pull her back down toward me and try to inhale all the soap in her hair. So that when Demetri sees her—if that's what he has been doing—he wonders where it has gone.

She begins to come regularly.

Over the next month and a half, I try to assess her depth. Sometimes I hear her on the phone with other artists she's trying to acquire. There's an undeniable scriptedness she enjoys tapping into:

"Good, good. Genius, Theo, and we can give you anything you need."

"We're just starting to take off, I don't know if that's . . . available."

"The reception will be in total silence. As part of the

work. To enhance the experience of the work. No voices." She paces around, warm, strident.

As she speaks, I remember one of the few times we met outdoors, in a park by the East River. Nati'd gotten there first. I saw her before she saw me—she was sitting on a bench, dressed in black, watching a group of young boys fight nearby. The fight was brutal. Nati did not intervene. She sat stiff and imperious, and she watched. I could tell she thought it was just the order of things. The boys knew she was watching. When they finished and began to slink away, they didn't necessarily approach her, but they angled their bodies toward her, to see if she might speak, sensing she held opinions about them and knew which of them had been close to glory.

Usually, though, we're in my apartment. And usually I've hidden a few things—like old photos of myself, chipped mugs I still use because I like the mouthfeel, the novels Demetri sometimes drops off for me, full of his marginalia. Then Nati arrives and the first thing I notice is her fabric—the chiffons and velvets and leathers draping, thinning her body in their collected looseness. And then immediately I'm squatting beneath her—painting or positioning her—and I see again the way her stomach comes up bladelike from her hips to her chest. I see the bottom of her eyes, their perfectly orbital shape, the way her eyelids collapse over them, sculpting them further.

I come to need her face in natural light. I make her stand

in silence in front of my window. I don't paint her. I just look.

In bed she's sometimes immaterial, sometimes the heaviest thing I've felt. When alone I find myself trying to actively reflect on what's happening between us or why or how it has happened—I almost don't believe it is happening, and I feel, somehow, and in a banal sense, disconnected from my own life just as I am most enthralled by it. But then I think of other things. My dishwasher is broken. My laundry is piling. Demetri has not been answering my calls.

Until, after five weeks of silence, it's late at night and he calls me. I'm alone. "Where have you been?" I ask him.

He tells me he's holding a vase hostage. His voice is breaking.*

"You're holding a vase . . . Is this a metaphor?" I ask him.

"No."

"What vase?"

"My neighbor's."

He tells me that for the past three days his neighbor has been in the process of moving out. She's been trekking up and down the stairs, to and from the lobby, carrying box after box. But now she's disappeared. A crystal vase has

---

**Breaking*, oil on linen, medium
A drop down a steep ravine. You will see it.

been sitting in the hall for the past couple of hours. "She's packing it last, probably," Demetri tells me. "She'll probably carry it on her lap, all the way to her new place. It's very nice."

"It sounds nice."

He tells me he's just been walking around his apartment, hearing the sound of the crystal shattering. "And now I am standing at the stairs, ready to drop it down into the lobby," he tells me.

"Demetri."

He's laughing. "There's that all-at-once sound. Broken bonds of the molecules, the sound of the pebbles scattering across the tile. Then the sound of sweeping them up. The hard shards, the edges scraping against the tile and the grouting."

"Okay."

"So do it?" he asks.

"Demetri. Put it down."

"I can say it was an accident. Actually, it will be an accident. I saw it outside her door. I was admiring it. I dropped it."

"Over the stairs?"

"I was holding it to the light."

"Put it down." I know how to hide the way my heart slams.

"I can't explain it to you. It's an itch, Ava, in my eardrum." I tell him, again, to put it down. "Okay," he says—

after two long breaths I hear the shatter all the way through the phone. "I put it down I put it down I put it down," Demetri says. "Shit. I put it down. I put it down." He begins to say something about Nati. I hear someone approach him through the phone. He hangs up.

THE NEXT NIGHT Nati and I are on my bed and she tells me her mother has been dying. She flips around and lifts herself onto her forearms. By now I have realized that Nati seems sometimes to think of internal reflection as a kind of gimmick or stunt of consciousness and not simply an ongoing, quiet given. Even her laughter, to me, has a certain hollow gloss. I watch her closely, the way she's moving her eyes. I consider how difficult it is to look at someone and know your premises are not the same. Nati goes on: "When I was little I would touch my mother's eyes, the wrinkled lids. And they scared me because they felt nothing like my mother. Like gelatin. Something made in a laboratory. But when I shoot her"—she'd been discussing her mother's impending death, how she's been demanding an assisted suicide—"I will have her close her eyes and I'll release her from them. Then I'll look in the mirror and find them on me. I will look so old."

She pauses again.

"And I'll be very relieved. She will be gone. I won't have to think of her sitting across from me at a restaurant in ten years, both of us older, her looking at me and thinking I'm aging. Her daughter has taken on the sag." Here I smile. I like when her phrases feel like they're making accidental sense. "My mother sitting there asking herself what has happened to her life. You must understand this." She's smiling at me. "Or you don't want to know any of this." She twists around, lies flat. "Why? You think knowing too much about me means you owe me something, Ava. Or I remind you of yourself. You feel unoriginal when you're with me. That's not so bad. Sometimes lives mirror one another." I don't answer. "You don't owe me anything." She's not talking about my piece for her gallery, though the remark makes me think of how I've yet to submit my portraits to her. I don't know who benefits from the delay. Maybe the value of my work will grow in the meantime and help her stature, or her value as a gallerist will grow, and her acquisition will help me. I'm sure she wants me to ask these questions. She likes to speak in transactions. My pride prevents me from engaging.

"You," she says, turning to me full-on, "you know you *could* be more curious. You don't even want to know about this? More about it?" She points to the scar under her belly button.

"I do know about you," I say. I tell her I know in her purse she carries an organized container of paper clips, needles, various scented sanitizers. "Vitamin E in case you scrape yourself," I add. "The straws." I tell her I know she is overprepared for tiny disasters. "And I think it's because what you really crave is a big one. Catastrophe."

"Oh!" She blinks at me and then props herself up so she is kneeling on the bed. "This is analysis, Ava." Her short hair bobs over her shoulders: "I want a big disaster. Nothing nothing nothing has happened to me. I'd like it if more could happen to me." And then she shrieks as she throws herself over my body.

(SOMETIMES, YOU FIND yourself lying down in the dead of night, thinking: I don't know what I've gotten myself into, and I don't like this part of my life. That's how I would explain this period.)

ONE DAY, SOON AFTER Nati told me I should be more curious, she arrives unannounced. I'm sitting thinking of Demetri—how I saw him the week before, pacing outside his apartment building. I mistook him for an insane person. He was stooped. His hair was unwashed.* He radiated violent silence—everyone around him hushed as they passed. I watched him and didn't call out to him. I panicked and turned around and left him. And now I'm wondering

---

**Unwashed*, acrylic on unprimed cotton canvas, large
Raw carnal browns. Layered and knotted beyond repair.

why, thinking of this in repeated cycles of anxiety, when Nati comes through my door, into my kitchen. She's wearing a soft gray overcoat. She has her hair pulled back tight and her face looks vivid and clean.

I make her coffee.

"Latte," she tells me.

I make one. I microwave the cold milk, froth it, pour it into diluted coffee—and bring it to her. She holds it with both hands. Her glass-black eyes are open wide. When the light hits them, micro threads of amber spool out from her iris.

She says she has an important question for me. She's sitting in the chair I like with her legs folded up. She asks me if I think I'm going to become as famous as they say.

"As who says?"

"The people who talk about you."

"Who is talking about me?"

She tells me how she was out, just last night. That she goes to these events and hears my name mentioned. There's talk of what I've sold, how inconsistent the sales are, but that it is impressive they happen with some frequency, that there's promise of the sales continuing. (I imagine this came up because I'd just been part of two group shows. For one, I constructed a series of wrinkled faces out of superfine copper wires. For the other, I streaked dry egg tempera onto bedsheets. Demetri wrote all the copy.) "But to me it's like you're too far under the threshold. You still have promise you've not exploited. But that's a good place to be. Do your best work while you're under there so you can fuck up when you cross it and no one will care. I'm there, too, in a sense." She sighs and crosses her legs.

"I'm too far under what? What threshold?"

"The blue-chip threshold. Just the general recognition threshold," she says. I look down. The problem is that I agree with her, of course, but also do not. "But," she continues, "if my gallery, I mean if Minni grows, I mean with you, and you give us something, which you will, I feel like we can take you there."

"Right," I say. I take this as her offer to eventually represent me permanently. I try not to react. She's not said it directly. She adjusts her chair and smiles. "So, I mean we can maybe grow together. And I can develop you, and you can develop the gallery in your way, and it will be a mutual act of growth, yes?"

The word *develop* sends me off a mental cliff.

"Right," I say. I pause and then I ask her, "Nati"—she looks at me, but I can't explain it. I have this vague, insistent sense that her comment is inspired by Demetri. That maybe they've been meeting. That maybe he's been explaining to her all of his criticisms of my work. One of which is that I never evolve an idea. I am too frenetic, move from theme to theme. I am scared to invest in an intellectually coherent project. I'm deluded in thinking hyper-proteanism and adaptability will make up for real rigor and depth. That what I need is a language and an ethics. I know these are his thoughts. I have the sense that maybe they are Nati's. I cannot ask and try to forget my suspicion.

"Sometimes your thoughts feel a little imported," I say.

"I'm all imported." She gives me a very Italian smile.

I suddenly grow defensive. I try to both obscure and clarify my thought: "I only mean that sometimes I can't tell if you mean what you say. Or if you even know what you mean when you say things. Or if what you say is yours."

Nati does not nod. She looks at me mean and clear. "I don't know." Then she stands and adjusts her skirt. I am still seated. Her body is two inches in front of me now, and I smell her warmth.

I find myself smiling because now, with her knees up by her chin, Nati looks very beautiful. And the simplicity of this makes me feel a certain dread, like I'm so full up with life I must be close to death.

"I told you I have a good eye." She's looking at me. "I mean sometimes I can even see you."

I put my hands over my face. She leans toward me and pulls them apart.

"Sometimes."

UP HERE ON MY STOOL I can see the edge of a canvas peeking out of my closet.

It's from last year. I painted it after returning from the bodega with Nati. She wanted peanut M&M's. I paid in cash. Standing at the register, Nati opened the candy. She emptied half the bag of M&M's into her mouth. "This is very good," she said, chewing with her mouth open. Inside, her tongue was brown and vibrant yellow and blue. She chewed and looked at me. I went home and painted her open mouth, the clotted colors, broken bits of shell clinging to the sharp edges of teeth.

I'M THINKING OF DEMETRI when he calls me. Nati is over.

"Where have you been?" I ask him.

"Working," he tells me.

"On what?"

"A little bit of everything." His voice* is so stern, so grounded in a certain reality, that I wonder if and where I've been living without hearing it. "I mean, I'm working for work, on Big Talk stuff, but also on my own stuff. I'm realizing," he says, "that's the only way to get it all done. I can't handle completely completing one task, then completely completing another. I have to break myself up bit by bit, getting a little bit of everything done every day. Terrible, but that's how it is and that's just what I'm doing." He

---

**Voice*, acrylic on canvas, small
A stern voice looks like this: full of flat horizon.

does not pause or give me room for questions. He is articulate. I'm convinced, briefly, that all indications of his delusion are merely symptoms of my own. "Are you, by the way, going to go to this party tonight?"

"No," I say. "I am not." But I had planned to. The party was for a friend of mine and Demetri's, who knew Nati through some other link. Nati was going and had asked me to go with her. I can tell by the way Demetri asks that he, too, plans to go.

"Okay," he says. "Well, I'm going."

"Okay."

"You're not coming with me?"

"You want me to come with you?" I remember Nati is in the next room, so I turn to face the wall. "I'm just surprised. You haven't called me."

"Well, you haven't called me," he says.

"Because you haven't."

"Well."

We're silent. I'm thinking of what to say that will get him to talk. I know he has been to two art talks recently where he spoke on my behalf. The crowd asked business questions—about what it means to make art in the context of a series versus individual pieces, if I worry about inflating the market with too many iterations of the same thing. I imagine the way he ceded "good points" and discussed the hopeful but precarious nature of my future.

"Ava?" he asks.

"Yes?"

"Have you seen her?" He means Nati. I search his voice for any hint of greater implication. There doesn't seem to be one.

I pause. "No, no." Have you? I want to ask. But we're silent again. I hear him sigh.

"Okay. Well, they were selling your weird Oreos"—a cookie that very much resembles an Oreo, but is not one—"I got you some. But I won't be seeing you tonight, then," he says.

"You won't be."

"So don't bring them?"

"Unless you want them," I say.

"I don't like them."

"Don't bring them."

"I'll bring them."

"Excellent." We laugh at nothing and hang up.

When I return to Nati she's lying down on the carpet. Her jacket is still on. I walk toward her and stand with my feet framing her ears. She begins to press her fingers between my toes.

"I can't go tonight," I tell her.

She stops pressing. "Why?"

"My brother wants to go."

"So?"

"So I'm sure he wants to see you." I study her reaction. Her face stays steady.

"You can't both go?"

"No," I say.

"Why?"

I don't answer.

"Why?" she asks again. I try to focus on her coat. There's bright yellow stitching to the right of the zipper line. "I can't talk to both of you?" She squeezes my pinky toe.

I nod but she can't see me.

"Ava." She gets up on her elbow. When I don't answer, she sits up. I follow the line across her brow and down her nose. "Are you going to make me ask again?"

"No."

"You're coming," she says. I stay silent. Her eyes are big. "So I've seen him. I mean we are friends. I'm friends with many people I don't talk about." She waits for me to speak. "You don't like to know these things. You're very insular. That's okay."

"Nati." The thing that's collapsing inside me—I don't know if it's for Demetri or for her or for my grotesque self.

"Tell me." She's laughing. "Tell me. What is . . . can someone only see one of you?" I don't answer. I don't know if she means she's seen him or been seeing him. I can't ask. "Interesting," she says. "Are you not allowed to be seen with me? In front of him?"

Somehow, I speak. "I'd just rather not."

"You'd rather not?"

I look at her. "I would rather not." I wait. "It would complicate things between us."

She looks me up and down. "Who is the us?"

"Between my brother and me."

Nati stands up. Her shoes make her taller than usual, but she bends so we're nose to nose, her eyes moving across my face. She takes her hand and puts it between my legs. "Ava"—she presses her index up into my groin and shifts tones—"are you not a big girl? You can't come out with me?"

When I don't answer she steps toward me. She opens up her jacket and begins to unbutton her shirt, then leans in, presses her chest against mine, and tilts her jaw to bite my neck. I don't move. "Ava," she says. When she steps back her face is blank before it begins to express some inner bleakness. Then it shifts again to express what I think might be confusion, but soon comprehend as accusation. I feel she is about to speak. The air-conditioning turns on. "Ava—" Breath catches in her stomach, and she emits this carnal pressure.

"Okay." She takes a slight step back. "Are you going to stand and make a fool out of me?" She laughs. We stand still until she puts her wrist to her brow. She pulls her shirt together and buttons it up to the neck. "Okay," she says, looking down at her fingers. "That's okay."

Before she leaves, she makes a point not to turn to me.

She puts on her coat and gives a brief smile to the counter, and then says nothing as she exits.

THAT NIGHT I KNOW they're both out. I don't hear from Nati. I think maybe she'll come over after. I lie in bed and imagine her walking into my apartment: she forgets to take her shoes off and so she hunches as if this will make her quieter. I imagine she comes to bed and lies down next to me, her breath smelling of liquor, lime, salt.

I think of her in a crowded room looking hard at Demetri. Her black hair pulled high over her ears. Her uneven eyes, looking in their split directions.

I close my eyes, open them, turn my body on its side, and think of her smiling at Demetri.

When he was a boy, teachers would keep Demetri in their classrooms at lunchtime and confess things to him. I used to imagine the way he must have sat there, listening in silence—attentive, innocent, knowing.* In paroxysms, I think of Nati telling him everything. What I've painted of her. The food I feed her. How well he'd take it. How he'd be more of a man for the ease of his understanding.

But then I shift. I think of her understanding me—or being calculating, I don't know the difference—I think of

---

**Knowing*, oil on linen, medium
This is an almost harmfully light piece.

her not telling Demetri a thing. Of her withholding everything with a naturalness that becomes her.

I feel my angst move around and no longer know where it belongs.

The next day no one calls me.

I stop by Demetri's apartment to stare at the door. I don't knock. I only listen for the sound of a home remodeling show that he only watches alone. I hear nothing.

A DAY OR TWO PASSES. Nati doesn't answer my calls. I walk around, nervous.

I'm realizing I don't want Demetri to find out because I don't want to be forced to test the limits of his understanding. And I don't want Demetri to find out because I don't want my extremely pragmatic and deliberate way of getting people to desire me revealed. I also don't want Demetri to find out because I do not want *this*, of all things, to be what gives him strength and rescues him out of his recent strangeness.

And I want Demetri to find out because I want him to know I am desirable. And I want to test his hate out on me. And because I think hate might help him to create something new.

I don't want Demetri to find out because I don't want him to ever suspect that I really wanted her without him. And then I wonder if this is true. I feel an unspeakable sense of embarrassment at not knowing exactly what love might be or what it means to experience it—whether or not I have, whether I can tell the difference between falling in love with someone and wanting to fall in love with someone because I want to believe it's possible for me. Again the sense of unreality settles in. Demetri is not there to dispel it.

THREE WEEKS GO BY and no one comes to see me.

When Demetri finally calls me, I try to keep my relief to myself. My toes curl in, I feel sweat collecting at my neck. He surprises me in the way he talks and talks. He tells me he hasn't called because he's been busy. He's been researching a lecture on the history of the railroad and why certain fish emit light. He tells me he wants us to go to Los Angeles. We need to visit our father, who had moved there ten years ago, for reasons related to his "restarting his life," and I'd yet to visit him. Demetri fills our calls with so many demands and hypotheses, and then hangs up. Then he calls back and asks me a series of questions: Did you paint the Fitz lobby? Did you begin your cuticle series? Did you send thank-you notes? Mail your checks to the studio? Are you leaving your apartment? Your doorman says papers are piling up outside, in the hall? Did you call the doctor about our skin tags? I answer everything, biting my tongue, waiting for him to shift tones and ask me questions I will not be able to answer.

(I'M LOOKING, NOW, at the pile of sketchbooks next to my microwave. I remember how when I was small, I walked into my bedroom and found my mother sitting at the edge of my bed. My sketchbook in her hands. She's flipping through it. She nods at the images. I stand in my doorway and watch her. I want to know which pages she's stopping on, which image she is running her fingers over. At one point she pauses, focuses, and I want her to show me what she has seen so that I might draw it for the rest of my life.)

SOON, I'M AT THE MUSEUM. It's six weeks since I've seen Nati. My general cluelessness has taken on a texture of its own. A fabric is over my mouth when I breathe. I am not working well. Demetri has not been in close contact, and nothing from Nati.

Wandering into the museum I see a large group of Midwesterners, there for a tour of the Temple of Dendur. I hear their accents, see their belts and bright, boxy cottons, and I find myself thinking of the night just before: I was in my apartment, I had thought of Nati to exhaustion and decided to go out. I put on my pink mesh top, twisted on my white pants, and matched them with blue slingback shoes. It was evening. I walked onto the street and felt the purple light hammer the massive downtown buildings into pastel cardboard slabs. I entered the bar at Greenwich and Seventh, where I often saw groups of men.

After settling in, I noticed one man who was smirking all the time, with his head down. He had buzzed blond hair, a broad face, his foot twitching. Ill-fitting blue jeans and a crumpled plaid shirt like a catalog gone wrong. I thought the men beside him were his company until they left him there alone. "Hi," I said, sliding onto the stool next to him. I had learned exactly how to be efficient. "Can I put this here?" I asked, putting my vodka in front of me and my hand on his leg. He said no. So did the others, that night, until it got so late that it became early, and I found myself drunk, my back roughing up against the brick wall of some utility building, my pants down at my ankles and a stranger so deep inside me I felt an ache at the base of my spine.

At the museum, the memory makes me stand up straight. I become mechanical. I charge forward and finally wind downstairs into a quiet rotunda. Suddenly I'm among the seventeenth-century Dutch. The rotunda is dark and warm. I walk around the curve. The massive, oiled faces gleam out at me. These faces—which have been hanging in one room or another for over three hundred years—are the freshest. So fresh that they are unfinished, as if the painter has just stepped away to brew tea, and I'm getting a preview of the wet paint. I convince myself I am alone with this wetness. That the young, sleepy housemaid is about to wake up, stand up, confess to me her dreams, confess to me her sins, before her creator returns. I convince myself that the laughter of a Dutch family—raucous around the table—is about to revolve briefly around this ugly stranger watching them, and then turn back immediately to themselves. Another glass will break, wine will spill.

Just when I start confessing to them, taking solace that they might not hear me, I sense someone behind me. It's a man I know, a friend named JT. He starts to talk to me. "I haven't seen you out," he begins. I don't want to speak. I try to usher out our conversation, and then he says: "I was wondering! Because that's what Demetri told me, picking up coffee. Two for Nati."

He goes on, something about how online sales were actually increasing.

"Two what for Nati?"

"Coffees. He, Demetri, had three cups in his tray." JT is smiling, and something in his look reminds me: he had witnessed us, Nati and me, on one of the few days we went outside together, to take a long walk straight down to Battery Park. We'd paused for a light and saw JT standing there, on the opposite corner of Hudson and Christopher. He watched us, waved, and didn't approach. "Demetri"—in the rotunda he goes on, his same smile—"Demetri said she liked two larges. And I did the mental math. That's nine dollars, four fifty for each large. Then whatever extra for Demetri's small. A whole joke somewhere about her being the only Italian who drinks Americanos." Now he looks at me like he wants me to clarify something for him. I don't move. He coughs. "But yes, so, they're saying the sales will even out, though, if galleries can get more foot traffic."

A man bumps me from behind.

"Fucking crowded," JT says.

But it's not. The man only brushed me, and I stay up. On the wall in front of us, an elfin girl's face attacks me. I feel sick at her pale skin. Her clay-white naked open eyes. Blood drains from my face. JT does not notice.

"Beautiful," he says, looking at the girl.

I nod. He asks me a question I do not answer and, thinking I'm taken by the girl, he lets me stand alone.

SOON AFTER THIS I find myself unable to work.

I convince myself everything will pass. I try to channel Demetri. I take a blank canvas and a black Sharpie and try to make a plan for the rest of my life. Nothing comes. I stare into the canvas—a woven white cotton—until its green underhues begin to show. Then I make a decision. I begin to draw a circle. Next I draw a square. I draw two parallel lines. In the upper right corner I draw what I'm pretty sure is a trapezoid. I begin on a rhombus when the phone rings.

Demetri: "I've been sick," he says.

"For how long?" I try to control my voice.

"A headache for a while. A cough for a day," he says.

"A day?"

"Two days, maybe."

"Are you eating?" I open my own fridge. Half an orange is congealing.

"Yes."

"Why haven't I seen you?"

"I'm working. It's a good thing."

I tell him I don't believe it. "Is there something on your face you don't want me to see?"

"No," he says.

"Anything bad to tell me? Show me?"

"Not that I can see," he says. "But you'd probably find something. You always look for things you don't want to see."

That evening I bring him spicy soup from Awang. Outside his door, I hear a voice in his living room, low and foreign. She's speaking quickly. I think perhaps she's had a breakdown before I realize she's speaking Italian. She's on the phone. The other person is on speaker, and the voice sounds like hers: loud, declarative, laughing. My spine grows cold. I try not to hear her. I pay attention to the voice on the other line. It must be a friend from back home. Then I hear children, small Italian voices. It must be her sister, her nieces.

I drop the soup. It doesn't spill, it lands perfectly upright. I move it close to the door.

THE VIOLENCE OF MY ANXIETY in this period cannot be explained. I will only admit here, to this page alone, that my most persistent anxiety involves a supreme selfishness: I wonder—if Nati doesn't want me, if this means I will stay underdeveloped. She said she would help me to grow. She made no promises to take all my work, but the implication was strong. This would have meant a bit of freedom. More money for my materials. A place to show with consistency. I will stagnate now. I will be unimpressive to Demetri but also to myself. I will not inspire the interest of others.

I try to talk myself out of this.

I try to say I'm better off. None of this matters. Nati is transactional. Nati is mercantile. Nati is interested in trade, not in art. Nati never said one thing—not one *real* thing—that convinced me of her aesthetic sensibility or sensitivity; that for all her decisiveness I wouldn't be able to tell you what she honestly *liked*. But then I think it's not true. The dark flash in her eyes at the sight of something beautiful. The unconscious viciousness with which she could express herself—a frank understanding of the stakes of existence.

She did not need to explain herself. This frankness is its own kind of art or special intelligence. But it's not enough. Something essential is lacking inside her. I felt the same suspicion while reading "notable" critics. They could think in sweeping categories, they could synthesize great quantities of information, but they let this broad vision obscure the individual, and one could see that their lack of imagination and courage to create for themselves was really their fundamental grievance. Anyway some core—I knew—was not occupied within her.

But then there was the promise that it might've been occupied, and I missed it. And now I have lost it. Then I wonder if Demetri was what was missing in her, and if now, in some twist, she is finally whole and ready for me.

Then, at last, I distrust her for ever having preferred me in the first place, if she did.

AT LEAST AFTER THIS the uncertainty stops coming in spasms and instead turns into a low-grade fever. So when Demetri calls me late on a Thursday—I am painting a white box onto a white canvas, an image of nothing—he tells me he's going to tell me something and that I am not to panic. I feel my lungs contract. All he says is he's planned the trip—we are going to Los Angeles to visit our father. This clears the path for me to think (or to pretend to think) of nothing but our travels for the entire next week. By which point we are already in California. Demetri is driving us along the Angeles Crest Highway.

I am nervous. I keep expecting him to make some subtle hint at what he knows. Or to tell me what has been bothering him, if he has dipped a little into madness. But Demetri's general and unexpected air of excitement relaxes me. At the Los Angeles airport he'd agreed to extravagances such as a nicer rental and extra parmesan sprinkled on his croissant. Now it's evening time. We're scaling the San Gabriel Mountains. Cold, long-limbed desert light is streaking the dashboard. Demetri's hand is loose on the wheel and I wonder if he and Nati ever drove together.

I'm falling asleep. But between closed-eye sequences I wake to see the same square of light on Demi's chin, like his jaw had been dipped in butter.* There's something on your face, I keep wanting to tell him. Before I can speak he comes in loud over the air-conditioning: "There was the day he"—he means our father—"told us about leaving," he says. "But I'm sure you don't remember that."

"Leaving where?" I manage. "The house?"

"Yeah," Demi says. "For Bright Life, if you remember, because he wasn't doing very well."

Demetri likes having a monopoly on memory. The moments he chooses to exclude me from always strike me

---

**Butter*, oil on linen, small
Nod of a chin dipped in butter but there is no yellow or really any brightness at all in this one and it looks weirdly violent.

as random exilings. It stunned us, despite his elusiveness, when our father said he was actually leaving. He'd told us it was just for a week. "A place called Bright Life." We were in the kitchen. He was talking low. I couldn't look at him. I stared at the calendar hanging on the wall behind his head. *APRIL.* I looked at the second row of blank squares. I looked at the row after that. Our father was still talking. "I need imagination. That was my mistake with your mother," he said. "That was what got her. I treat people the way *I* want to be treated. That's a mistake. It was my mistake, with your mother . . ." His rambling was leisurely. He said he felt comfortable leaving because he knew we, unlike him, had imagination in abundance—and so he used his imagination to figure that we didn't quite want or need him right now. If he was going to better himself, it would have to be in complete solitude, with no additional pressures. He said it to both of us, but while only looking at Demetri.

Not more than two nights away and he came home. Bright Life only had so much space, he told us, and they needed people who were truly broken. Demetri believed him. I did not. I thought he missed the sense of our mother in our home. Her smell, her hair in the dust. I wanted him to confess his real reasons to me. I tried to talk with him. I followed him into his bathroom where he stood shirtless and oddly strong. He began to floss his teeth. Before I said anything, he spoke: "I know, Ava," he said. But then he said no more. I wondered if he was suspicious—if he thought I was trying to extract from him some marrow or inner element that could not be put back.

Because of course I was. I wanted him rid of it. The ongoing, unredeemed grief embarrassed me.

In the rental, which Demetri is driving with aggressive caution, he explains what he keeps calling our father's "situation." "Because you've never asked," he reminds me. Because of his lack of income, our father's house in LA is subsidized by a combination of charitable sources, most of all the state. He quit writing commercials and is spending his days in relative comfort and dereliction. Demetri knows this because he has seen him over the years. We've never discussed his visits. I would have given our father money had he asked for it. But I knew that at random intervals Demetri sent him checks signed with both our names.

Nominally, we were in California because Demetri said he had been asked by Big Talk to go and watch one of their clients speak—a talk about perseverance at a local college. But it also happened to be our father's birthday.

"Maybe he'll be bearded," I say.

"Maybe. He likes plants now."

I look out the window toward the houses on the cliffs, slung low and flat, all-glass ranch styles. I ask if our father's house is nice.

"No."

"Plants sound kind of nice."

"You'll see. It's like a bungalow. Kind of dark. He doesn't move much."

"Who waters the plants?" I ask.

"I assume he does."

"And if he doesn't?"

"I don't know." Demetri smiles. "Why do you want them to be dead?"

The curves are long and steadying. "Is he obese?"

Demetri doesn't answer.

"Oh my god," I say.

"Ava."

Seen from the outside, our father's house is all right. The driveway is integrated into the steep decline of the street. From the lawn all you can see is one horizontal roofline. A small turbine sticks out of an asphalt shingle. "A turbine!" Demetri says. We both notice it's a little unhinged. "That's new!"

The front door is unlocked. Inside there is one large room, with the kitchen toward the back end, and to the right, immediately after walking in, there is one bedroom, where my father lies.

It's not the disordered rooms that disturb me, or the scent of wet towels and bleach. Nor is it the shallow, dome ceiling; the sensation of being cupped under a plaster bubble. It's that the man I find lying on the bed in the one windowless bedroom, that man is not my father, but Demetri. I am convinced. It's Demetri lying there, lean-bodied with eyes calm and open, lips chapped. It's Demetri who tells me to duck my head so I don't bang it against the potted golden pothos hanging from the ceiling. And it is Demetri who instructs Demetri and me to sit down—not on the chair, but on the bed itself, so he can see us better. My eyes hurt from the strain of double vision. In my mind Demetri's look-alike had always been our mother. She'd given him her hair, the fraught eyes. But looking at my father. Old man. His jaw, chin, the weight of skin against bone, the faint groove between his brows. The direction of the folds around the eyes, as if gravity was hitting Demetri and him at the exact same degree. The clean, cluttered set of teeth . . . I calm down and expect clarity when I refocus, only to again look at Demetri and feel my father locked inside his face, and then to look at my father and feel Demetri scratching underneath him.

"Hi, there, Ave." Our father smiles up at the plant hanging above him. It's overflowing: two stems sprawl out to the left, and one spirals right down to his chest, where it curls around itself, ending in a loop just big enough for him to put his head through. "You're too skinny."

I'm going to say something when Demetri looks at me, pleading.

"Hi, Dad."

There is a moment of pause before our father nearly yells: "We won't make it dramatic! Come! Come!" But we're already so close. I see the grease on his chin.

I look again at Demetri, who is not looking at me, and then ask our father about the house. When, exactly, he had moved in. Whether the humidity was what ruined the wood in the walls, on the floors.

"It's a desert," Demetri reminds me. "So it's dry here."

"That's very good, Demi, that's exactly right." Our father nods and then turns to me. "But there is a little rot outside, right at the hose faucet. It leaks." He looks again to Demetri, and his face seems to suggest this is some intriguing new game, looking from one child to the other.

I ask him who does his grocery shopping, why he is in bed, if he has friends in his area. He says he does it himself, he is exhausted, he has a friend named Sugar two houses down. "That's nice of you to ask, Ava. Yes. She brings me things, I borrow her ladder. She's given me eggs. Sometimes if I'm baking bread, which I do, because you need some standards and customs, because that is life, and sometimes I'm baking it and need yeast"—he winks too hard—"I get a rise out of her."

He asks about New York, about what Demetri has been working on, about what kind of food we eat. He makes sure that I'm still painting, as if he doesn't know that it is my life, and so I exaggerate, telling him I've had many solo shows.

"Yes? I've never seen one! It's hard to see things when you're stuck in this little room." It is unclear to me to what extent he is actually stuck. "Have you ever had a show in

Los Angeles? The world doesn't just come to you." He looks meaningfully at us, first me, then Demetri. "I mean, until it does. But that's so great, Ave," he says. Demetri smiles at me, trying to double my father's goodwill. "You know," our father goes on, "I was thinking before you arrived about how I'd hate to have one of those horrid conversations, where I tell you how much more I'd have liked to take care of you. How I wish I could have given more of myself to you both. All that sentiment . . ." For a moment he lifts his hands. My father's body must be burning under his blanket. I realize I can't tell where exactly his legs are, where his hips end, how any of him is composed, and I convince myself that underneath his blanket he is completely mutilated. A congealed mess of raw blood and bone. I think of how I'd paint this. I'd put thick red on a mop brush. Piss-tinted yellows for the exposed layers of fat. "But you know, I really—and I don't know what this says about me, that it was so little—but I really did give you everything. I mean all that I had. It's just when all of you isn't enough . . . that kind of thing . . . I hope you can understand that. We're not going to expand on it."

I remember a novel Demetri gave me—in one section the narrator discusses how one comes to take pleasure in the pain of one's toothache, how one's moans become luxurious, thickened by one's witness to one's own anguish. I realize this is what my father reminds me of.

Demetri nods. I watch all the veins in his neck. "Of course."

"I mean what you need to understand, I suppose, at the very least, is that if there were more resources I would have given them to you. If I had had more, you would have had it. Sometimes success is an accident"—he looks at me—"and sometimes failure is an accident, too."

"Right." Demetri nods again.

"You can see here"—he gestures around him—"that I have mostly nothing. I hope you can see that. Not that I'm destitute. Obviously I have the essentials. I am never wanting for anything material. I am always well-fed. But for a while I thought I might save money, get something nicer, work my way out. It helped me to think of you two gallivanting around New York. Thinking of you free. Though of course you two had your issues, I'm sure. And remember, when you were younger I sent you those checks. When you were what, seventeen? Eighteen? Up in Boston?" Here he looks at us like he's caught us in a lie. "I hope you remember that I sent you checks often. Money from the royalties." The royalties were for a commercial he made for a multivitamin, starring our mother. "I sent them to you once every two weeks. I'm sure of it because I remember coming up with little scenarios in my head, of how you two might react when the checks came. I was a little sick back then. Still, I'd wonder how you thought of me, far away, yes, but always thinking of you. How maybe you thought of me sitting down to write them. And I wondered what you thought when you saw my handwriting. If you thought: I love the way he writes our names, with the *D* like that. That's just like him to put the *AVA* in all capitals, like it's the beginning of a prayer, like I've always told you, Ava. I wanted you to feel me in them. It made me happy to write them. Ask the nurses." He says this like they are still on hand. I turn around. He laughs.

"That was the happiest moment of my day. I'd be in the middle of something, and I'd remember: the children need the checks. Of course, you weren't children anymore, you could've taken care of yourselves. But still. I'd drop everything I was doing. And it became such an event. But when the royalties ran out . . ."

"Royalties don't run out," I interrupt. Demetri glares at me. "I mean they're royalties. They're with you for life. They're loyalties." I try to smile.

"That's right," our father says. None of us speak. "Well, that's great then." He clasps his hands over his chest and appears to calm down. I keep trying to make hurried contact with Demetri, who is going out of his way to focus.

"Well enough about the checks. I'm finding, you know, actually, that memories are cropping up. Which is what you get when your past comes in. Not that it's your fault. Not yours at all. Demetri, sit back down! Ava is comfortable."

Demetri does as told.

"So, have you two fallen in love or anything?"

I stay still. Demetri clears his throat.

"Obviously I mean with other people."

Nothing.

"Well, that's good. That's distracting stuff, right?" He pauses, sighs, and then a certain boyish paternal quality creeps into his speech: he begins telling us that there is work to do around the house—he is glad I've pointed out the wood rotting, because that is one place that needs fixing. The other is all the chipped paint. And it is getting dusty on the floor. Not everywhere, but in the corners of the house that are not quite visible, so there is the sense of a mildly accumulated weight that disturbs him. He is wondering how long we plan to stay. "Because if you do plan to stay awhile, I know there's only one other room in here, but Sugar has another room at her place. And so one of you could stay here, and the other at Sugar's. Or, if you'd like, Sugar could come stay here, and you two could go to Sugar's . . ."

"Well, Demetri has an event tomorrow morning," I say. "So we're just stopping by tonight."

"Yes," says Demetri. "Though Ava is not coming to the event."

"How's that?"

He repeats I am not coming to the event.

"I'm not *in* the event. I'm just going to the event," I say.

"You're not allowed at the event. I mean you don't have a ticket. And it's sold out."

I feel our father watching us.

"Okay." I leave it.

Our father smiles in a way that makes me cough. "I wasn't going to mention it, Ava, but what I think Demetri is trying to say, I *think*, is that since you didn't come with my birthday present, apparently you still have to paint it."

"HE'S REQUESTED IT, AVA. He asked for it. On the phone. Weeks ago. He's been planning to have it." On the drive to our hotel, Demetri confirms that the next day he will leave me in our room to paint. He speaks with a defensive edge: "If I had told you, you wouldn't have come. And if I had asked you to make something beforehand, for me to bring him, you would have said no." I don't deny this.

I want to tell Demetri that my intuition is that our father only plans to sell it. I also think of asking whether Demetri believed our father when he implied he hadn't really heard of my work. Or if he was simply hoping for a big reaction. But I don't want to be mistaken for caring about the answer.

"And what am I supposed to paint him?"

"Anything you want. Return to your roots. Paint him a plant."

Before reaching the hotel we find a strip mall where a

craft store is tucked between two empty gyms. Demetri stays in the car as I run in to buy cheap paints (basic studio acrylics, a set of six colors), a set of red sable brushes, a double-primed canvas stapled on standard strips. I figure instead of an easel I can prop the canvas on a hotel room chair, or lay it flat on the floor. At the register I buy a newspaper to spread across the carpet.

"Okay," I say, entering the car.

I STAY UP THINKING. Only in the morning does the image come to me—it's a memory of a painting wherein two women stand and stare at each other. I used to see the women every day, framed on the door to our high school art room. A creamy, level lilac runs like a vein between their two bodies. Both women are composed of circles and orbs: The left woman's breasts are pinned on like scrota. The other woman's breasts are separated and float like moons. For whatever reason I always thought of the women as a mother and daughter pair. Maybe there was something fertile, maternal, in the yellow: a smooth, yolky yellow, cut into diamonds behind their bodies. At some point I was corrected: the painting is actually of a single woman looking into a mirror, staring at her reflection.

For my father I re-create this. Only I go back to my original mistake in perception, make things filial—my father looking right at Demetri, in a double portrait of sorts.

The issue is that Demetri's face is still off-limits to me. I have to be subtle. I decide to place him on the left side of the canvas. On the right side, my father. Both of them in profile, both of them composed of shapes and patterns, trapezoidal cheeks, cylindrical necks and ears. I am suddenly grateful I've been practicing my little geometries. I make their profiles the same, except my father's nose has a sharper beak since over time more fat has shed off the bridge. I use greens. I think of the spiral of my father's plants and connect their bodies using interlocking tendrils. Behind them, I let black paint work like a cosmic force pressing them forward.

The next morning, when Demetri arrives back at the hotel, he mentions nothing about where he slept or what happened at the Big Talk speech (later I'd learn there was no speech at all, that he'd come to Los Angeles to collect footage for his film about us). Instead he beelines* for the canvas. I wait for his critique, suspicious that he might see himself and rebel.

Demetri lifts the canvas over his head and walks to the window so that the sun can shine behind the linen and expose all the mistakes in gradation of color and consistency of form. I know he is going to call out the values in my green—the paint did not lend itself to a variety of density,

*__Beelines__, acrylic on mac and cheese cardboard box, small
Is a mac and cheese box "small"? Maybe it should be "medium-small"?

it all screamed at the same pitch. But Demetri only puts the painting against the wall and takes out his keys.

I NOTICE, OF COURSE, that we haven't mentioned Nati's name. I haven't thought of her, and yet when I do return to her I know I had to have been thinking of her because she is now a film—a thin membrane spread evenly over my consciousness. I don't need to recall her with clarity, because I am recalling her vaguely at all times. But then in other moments, when she does occur to me—her face, her walk—I look at Demetri to see if he has parallel thoughts, as if at the exact same time we might feel ourselves trapped under the same current.

WHEN WE RETURN to our father's he is in the same position as before: on the bed, surrounded by foliage and an abundance of pillows. When he sees us, he clears his throat and wipes his mouth with his arm. "Children," he says, "today you leave!"

I do not make a show of handing him the canvas; he knows it's coming. I do worry, with his tubular arms, about his ability to hold it upright, but Demetri is already behind it, using his palm to support the frame.

Our father is silent with the painting for some time. He observes it carefully. Demetri looks at him with such silent expectation that I nearly tell him to quiet down. Although I, too, am nervous. It's the first time my father has really looked at anything. The first time he's been asked to comment. And always, not until people begin to scrutinize your work do you perceive the depth of its faults. I want to take it away.

My father tilts the canvas away from his face and looks up at me. "There are some very pretty colors in here, Ava," he says. "Those colors are so nice."

"Oh," I begin, but Demetri beats me.

"Do you see," he says. "It's—do you see you are here, I mean here—" Demetri swivels to face the canvas and is about to point.

"I don't need—" our father begins; he tilts the work away from Demetri, softens his tone. "I really don't need you to tell me." He waits. Demetri looks at me. I find myself wondering what Demetri has told Nati of our father. *After all, he's a good man*, I hear him saying.

Our father begins to laugh and starts to prop himself up so he might get out of bed. I prepare myself for his mutilated legs. "It's as I'd expect." We wait as he slowly uncovers himself. "You two think I don't get it." I hardly have time to register how fully formed he is. When he stands it is with such strength and balance I begin to feel afraid. I remember against my will the pride I'd felt as a child walking beside him.

He staggers around the bed, leaves the room, and walks

toward his kitchen. Demetri comes around and grabs onto my arm. Together we follow him toward the back door.

"Children are always thinking this about their parents. That their parents do not get it." He's trying not to laugh. "The sisters in *King Lear*—remember that your mother played one of them—they think their father is a goner. Cronus castrates his father." Our father pit-pats around his kitchen. "And my children think what? That I'm a narcissist. Tell me, Ava, was it conscious, this painting? Or did you not realize what you had created until you were through? Because you were in a state of obliteration?" He is quoting a combination of what Demetri and I have said in my interviews, and I think to myself, Okay, so you *do* know me. "Ava," he continues, "you think I'm self-obsessed. I mean, this is what you're telling me. Yes?" I know it's a good time to tell him that he is not looking only at himself in the painting but at Demetri and him. It is a double portrait. I meant to convey a relationship. It occurs to me, however, that Demetri must have also thought it was my father looking at his own reflection. I realize I've failed at something I now can never explain. I also realize the human eye will choose to see a mirror before all else. "That's why you've left me alone," he went on, "or maybe it was for protection. I mean for my protection"—he clears his throat—"since you're afraid you might kill me, after having killed my wife."

He pauses. Looks at Demetri, then at me, then back at

Demetri. Then he breaks out laughing. Please stop, I want to say. He tilts his head back and puts his hand on his stomach. As he leans, I see his crotch press through his boxers, a sack of something soft and sad. "I'm only fooling you!" he says. "Of course I'm just teasing. But look at you two!" He gestures toward us. Demi's hand is still hot on my arm.

"So cute! God, you two are the cutest. The way you just stick together. I remember that. Everyone told me you were the cutest kids. The mothers knocked on my door to check in, after your mother. Until they stopped. But it helped to have Demetri always so well-behaved, everyone said it, like every moment of his life was this miracle of behavior. That's what they told me. Of course, none of them knew that he truly was a miracle. Because he almost died, the one time. Nowhere indecent, you know. Not at a Kroger. Just out in the backyard, in the snow. We left him out there for too long"—our father is talking to no one now—"because we stepped inside for a moment and in that moment your mother wanted me. And when she wanted me she wanted me. She put her hand on me. How Demetri has his hand on you now. She put her hand on me and gave me that look where she pursed her lips and opened her eyes wide, lips so soft, *Hi.* And Demetri was still playing outside because there was a snowstorm. We could still hear him laughing. We thought he would be fine. He had to be fine, because inside the house, your mother wanted me, and then she had me, and when it was over I went outside by myself to find him. And he was gone. The yard was all white. Until there was a shifting nearby, and I saw the bluest thing of my life, which was the top of his little hat. He'd buried himself. I picked him up. He was stone-cold in my arms. His ears were purple and pulpy, dripping ice.* He had put icicles in his ears, and they'd melted and flooded the canal. And when I lifted him and dusted off all the snow I realized he was not speaking and that his lips were not purple but black. And so I took him to the hospital, and they told me that in all likelihood he'd be very damaged. Something to do with his hearing. Also his brain. So it was a miracle he ended up talking. And soon, after talking, he began excelling. All the prizes. Really a miracle. Though I do remember . . . and it's horrible . . . I remember wondering . . . I do admit to wondering . . . if I was asked at the gate of hell—would you take back that moment with Marion, so that your son never risked injury . . . I'd say no." Demetri lets go of my arm to fix his collar, puts it back. "I'm fucking *kidding* about before! About killing your mother. Not to say I don't have theories. But a part of me thinks you two came here to be hurt together, so I'm trying to do that, I guess. To succeed in at least something for you." This time our father shouts. "You didn't mean to *hurt* her. You can relax about that. I did, of course, fail her

---

**Ice*, oil with gold leaf on linen, small
I soaked my fingers in an ice bath to try to re-create the texture of pruned skin. My fingers were still numb when I finished the painting. You can tell.

worse than both of you. In the everyday kind of way. In the banal way, which is the worst way to hurt someone. And then you try to talk to her when she says she feels funny—like both hollow and heavy and whatever the hell else—and you try to help, but all expressions sound sour coming out of your mouth, because they've been said before—they exist in bullet form on a database, or on a poster in a waiting room. Your consolations are for someone else, they're not the words you have for her, because the real words for her are in some beyond, probably the same beyond you reach in death, after they're useful, and so in a way that's what you pray for: for both of you to die so you can finally tell her what you mean. But your children are in the next room. So in the meantime you just tell her you understand, you understand, you understand. Though soon you realize not everyone likes to feel so thoroughly understood—do you two know what I mean?"

He runs back into his bedroom and comes out with a broom. As he holds it up straight, I can see through his knuckle into bone. "Do you want to know why I really had to leave?" He pauses.

Demetri starts to speak. But our father continues: "It happened, if you remember, that your mother was very good at two things: chess and indigestion. Often they happened at the same time, so that when she was halfway through a game with me—and you remember, we played." He waits for Demetri and me to nod. We both remember.

"When we were playing together and she was winning, she'd get up, turn on the radio, and say, 'No cheating,' and would leave the room for a half hour, sometimes longer. Well, so, one time she came back from the bathroom. She stared at me, and said she thought the board looked different. I still remember, she thought I had moved her rook from d4 to b4. I knew her moods by then, of course. Although only when her arms began to crack from the scratching did I become serious about calming her down, whatever that meant. 'Just tell me you did it,' she repeated, 'please tell me you cheated.' It was slow, and then sudden. She threw her arms at the board. She demanded I admit it. Of course, I would not. That's rule number one." He looks from Demetri to me. "Right? You never admit to something you didn't do."

We nod.

"So I denied it. And she began to scream. She tore around the house, scraping against the walls, turning off the lights. And so I stood still. Don't try to touch her, I thought. She stayed in the living room, and I stood still in the kitchen. I kept counting to ten—one, two, three . . . thinking at some point we'd both be delivered elsewhere. Or that I'd count myself to sleep. I'd wake up from her breath on me."

I realize my father might have taught me how to love.

"And just when I thought I sensed a silence from the other room, when I prepared to go to her, she burst out again, calling me a weak man, this and that. She went into our history. How I'd failed to turn her into something. Into anything. How horrible this was. How I'd never know. How I had no talent. Or not enough. This and that." He smiles. "Eventually, of course, she calmed down. I don't know when. I was sitting when she came to me. Probably half asleep. It was as I'd imagined it, or better. She put her hands on my shoulders. She made me open my legs so she could stand between them, and then put her forehead down to meet mine, and we were inside her hair and she was breathing slowly. She told me that she had rehearsed the game in her head many times. Every move. She'd gone over the whole thing. She told me I was right. I had not touched her piece. She was sorry. She loved me. I told her I understood. She promised to trust me completely from then on. She apologized again and again, until the apology itself became a kind of paranoia that I worried might take her away." He pauses, lifts the broom, and puts it down three times. "Anyway, it didn't. The camera—which I bought—was to be used each time we played chess. It was one of the first little camcorders ever made. Your mother acted surprised each time I brought it out, like it was my preference and not hers. I'd set it up on a tripod between us before each game. At times she looked right into its lens. She posed for it in subtle ways. Even when it was off. That was the worst. That even the illusion of being captured was enough."

He begins to lose himself. Then, newly energized: "I

didn't film our entire game, of course. Only myself, alone, when she went to the bathroom, so that she would have footage if she ever suspected something. And then, when she died, I had the urge, sometimes, to go through and look at all the footage I'd collected. All the minutes—hours, in total—of me waiting, alone, for her return. I knew I'd find myself just sitting there. Waiting. Just sitting. Looking dumb. With a half-played game of chess in front of me. She'd be gone so long, and I'd be so still, that it became a kind of meditation, and I'd forget I was being recorded at all."

Our father pauses. He's standing beside a bowl of plums. From no force but the pressure of brief silence, the top plum rolls off the counter and onto the floor. I go to pick it up. The void of Demi's hand tears a hole on my skin, and I regret moving. I don't know where the garbage is, and do not plan to ask, so I hold the plum in my hand, drill my finger into its bruise, breaking the weaker fibers and hitting the pit.

"Ava," our father says, making clear I've diverted his attention. But I know he will return to his story. His digressions are power plays. "Ava was smart because she liked to go to the museums. Good children! And when she drew perverse things, it was evidence of either a depth of mind or a serious disorder, but both flatter the parent so long as the disordered child is some kind of savant. But it *could* have been debilitating, Ava, because you listened to your brother"—our father takes a moment to cough, letting his temples swell—"who screamed at your mother's belly, 'GET OUT!!! GET OUT GET OUT GET OUT!' She listened." He looks at Demetri. "One month early. It could have been bad. But she listened, and it worked out. And she's listened to you ever since then. Everything you say. Is it still true? Demetri? I'm sure it's still true. Things like that don't change. She listened to you. She pretends not to but it's all she does. But you, Demetri, you know, you seemed to form opinions only so that she could attach herself to them. Neither of you are free, do you see? But I'm sure you already understand that." Demetri and I don't look at each other. "And your mother felt it, you know, the obedience between you two, her children, the secret little alliance. And then, she started telling me . . ." He looks at us. "She started telling me there was a death in the family." His eyes turn only to Demetri. "But, Demetri, she only meant you were growing up and were only a fraction less interested in her, and really that *she* had died. I mean that a part of her had died. She said having your full attention was like being covered in light, was like being on camera. And that when you left her, Demi, I mean when you showed a certain reluctance, it was like living for no one. And because we lived in a small town, where I'd brought us, and there was no one around to observe her, I knew she was right. And I watched her become obsessed, a bit more possessive over you, Demetri, and I did nothing about it, because it was clear to me that when she was with you, she was fully living. And sometimes I thought about when I found you out in the snow, how she stayed inside. I went out to look for you, found you buried, and she stayed inside. She told me not to go check on you, that it was okay because we could hear you laughing, even though we could not, and how she could have let you die. And sometimes I wonder if she was trying to tell me she was ready to go, too. That if she'd have let you go, it meant she was ready, too. But I would not ask her about this, you understand . . ."

He pauses. He'd slowly begun to hunch through his speech but now stands up, called to duty. "So! I promised myself I'd never watch the tapes. It was all just footage of me, alone, of course. That's all it was. No reason to watch them, nothing in them but myself. But then she was gone. I mean into the Sound, you know." He looks at us. "And the tapes were sitting there. I knew exactly where they were. And as I looked at them tucked in their plastic boxes, I thought maybe they'd show *more* than just me sitting and waiting: I thought maybe she'd appear in them, by surprise. A glimpse of her rising, or of her sitting back down. Or of her calling to me as she made her way through the hall. I thought maybe my memories were all wrong and that there was laughter every now and again. Maybe she'd tripped one day and fallen down laughing. And maybe I rose off my chair and went to lift her, and we talked, and the camera heard us, or caught the edge of my spine as I pulled her off the ground. And so, ten or so years later, I put in the tape. I saw myself sitting there, waiting for her, and I suppose I experienced what we spend our lives trying to prevent, which is to say I saw what I will look like when I die, what I will look like if I'm very scared when I die. Because the tapes showed me sitting in that chair looking like I'd died a very slow, frightening death." He leans back to laugh. "And that is, in part, why I left, briefly, for Bright Life. Because I knew you had two dead parents. One in the ocean and one in the house. I couldn't do that." He smiles and taps on the counter three more times, and then turns to face me before he pitter-patters back into his bedroom to retrieve the painting.

"Anyway, I didn't stay away. Too weak to stay away. And Ava saw that." He gestures to the painting. I wonder, watching him, with a sense of shock and also a certain sense of banality, what the world is for if people can never quite know one another. "And so that's what's here, Ava?" he says, returning, holding the painting in his arms like a fat child. "You've seen it. Do you see what I mean when I say there's nothing I could have done. I was always already seen, as they say. You had already found me! You had found me even back then. I remember how you looked at me, you were maybe seven years old, your teacher came over, remember? About the school. And you looked at everyone at the table, but the way you looked at *me*. I knew it then—I could not look back at you for long because you had a joke in your eyes that was intolerable to me. And since I have no one to look at me anymore, I'm stuck looking at myself. Which you capture here quite well." He pauses. He looks down. "I don't remember," he says. "I can't remember. Maybe I did cheat. Maybe I wanted to see what would happen. Maybe I wanted to test her. Or I wanted to win. A man likes to win. I don't remember. Maybe I did cheat. I don't know." I watch him swallow. "Anyway, it doesn't matter. It does not surprise me, Ava. You have always sniffed for weakness. I mean, even back then you would find it in a person and then would observe it quietly, and you'd understand how to draw it out. And maybe a part of me, my whole life, has been wary that whatever was needed to turn those observations into . . . what? I don't know. To turn them into a kind of . . . finality. A kind of final, fatal statement . . ."

I realize Demetri is no longer beside me—in fact, he is no longer in the room. I let go of the plum in my pocket and hold my stomach. "It's all so ridiculous," our father goes on. "Do you see it's dark in here, now?" It isn't dark. The sun is only halfway down the trees. Our father comes toward me. Demetri comes back into the room.

I don't like scenes. Demetri likes them less. Before I can process his face, I feel myself being pulled into the foyer, then out the front door. I wonder if this is an overreaction. It doesn't seem to matter. When we start to turn around our father begins to laugh once more. He leans against the counter. "Okay! See you guys!" His voice is strong, his face red and disfigured, the way Demetri gets when he sings. Though our father is only smiling.

We hustle up the driveway, to the car. I hear myself breathing. Demetri's door opens but mine does not, and as he stands there trying to find the unlock button, I turn to look at my father's roof, where—I notice—the turbine, already semidetached, has slid down and caught on an upturned shingle. I think of knocking on my father's window. I don't know what not having a turbine might mean for him. I imagine mold vining its way up his ceilings, mildewing his towels. I imagine his plants wilting, a stalk's shriveled inward swirl tickling him in the night as he chokes. I think of yelling out. Before I can decide what to do I hear the car lock lift and pull at the door.

In the car Demetri and I are quiet. When I look at him, he manages to look annoyed at my looking at him without returning my gaze, tilting his head at minute degrees as he chews his cheek. I wonder if he's thinking about how he'll explain it all to Nati, as she sits listening to him, working her way through her coffees. We near the hotel. At our final turn Demi starts to shuffle around. I think he's about to begin a speech of his own—a rebuttal, or at the very least an assessment. I even start his speech in my head. *Ava*, Demetri will tell me, *I actually think overall that went well. We had to see him together. He confirmed what we know to be true. He was actually surprisingly spry, and very articulate, once he got out of bed. There were some* *insights there that reassure me. And at least we know he's still cinematic . . .* We pull into the lot and Demetri shuffles once more, and then lifts his right thigh and farts* with such aggression that I feel his seat rattle. The end of the stream turns up like a question mark. In our usual pattern, we are silent before we crack open, laughing in long, breathless winds. I realize we sound like we are choking. Dying. It makes me laugh harder. Demetri's eyes are watering by the time we park the car.

He unfastens his seat belt and opens his door, swinging out his legs. Under his seat, I can see into the bottom of his bag. There's a scattered array of tapes, labeled in our father's handwriting. But we are too limp, now, and I don't ask.

IN THE TWO WEEKS after this trip to our father's, Demetri does not call me. In the meantime I convince myself to stop thinking about calling Nati—but then a warm afternoon makes me wonder what she looks like outside, sitting with a straw pinched between her lips. I've not been working well and have convinced myself she is the reason. I give in and she answers. I can't think of anything to say.

**Farts*, texturized joint compound on canvas, medium
You can make swirly patterns in joint compound (think of a texture kind of like wet clay) by using a metal comb. I tried to capture the swirl of the fart and hope you can hear it.

"Hello?"

"Hi, this is Ava." Demetri did not mention you once on our trip, I want to tell her. And I've been curious: Why? Understand that I want to know everything. I can take it. I want to know. The whole point, actually, is me knowing everything, so I can make something of it. Maybe knowing will get me to work. Is it too healthy to risk bringing around me? To risk telling me? Its wholesomeness might pain the most, yes, but I could take that, too.

Instead I simply breathe.

She waits. "Yes, I do know that."

"I just want to know if maybe Demetri knows anything about us, for any reason. So that I know how to act, what to do."

"What do you mean?"

"Like if you told him anything that happened between us?" I don't tell her about my dreams, how he has been accusing me, and the spiral I've fallen into—where I feel I might be deluding myself into thinking he'd care at all.

"What happened between us?"

We're silent for a minute. She has to go.

"Of course."

I hang up and try to convince myself the rest of my life will take place, with or without me. I paint more portraits of Nati. I use my small brushes so the process takes longer. The problem is that I cannot sell this work. I am running out of money. My prideful aversions to careerism, even to professionalism, are closing me in. I shut down the requests for virtual art contributions. I'm not smart enough to conceive of anything medium-specific (where there's a real reason for the art to be on a screen and not on a canvas, other than maybe it flashes and turns). A message in my inbox, from a new art collective, reads: *If you've been looking for a way to advance your status at the expense of your ethics, join us.* What would Demetri say? Again I play his voice in my head. He'd launch in with a heightened academicism: *Chronic irony is only an expression of the fear of beauty, the fear of being moved. It is an attempt to preempt the self, to never be unknowable to oneself, because with irony one knows everything beforehand, and debases it. But we all must stay unknowable to ourselves, at least a little.*

Unknowable to myself—that is what I'm becoming, but only in the sense that I begin to feel less like a person at all. I try to form something new in my brain. The way to do this is to engage with other people's art. But I can't go to the museum. I can't go to galleries. I don't know why. Instead, I try to read a few of the novels Demetri left me. They're still hiding under my couch. He feeds on the canon. I pull out *The Brothers Karamazov*, *The Portrait of a Lady*, *Giovanni's Room*. On each page I lose focus trying to untangle Demetri's marginalia, which floods every border and seems embedded with its own plot. I put the books down and go over again how I might come to some kind of conclusion.

And then my phone rings.

"Ava." It's Demetri. "I was thinking. I think I'd like a party."

In a month he's turning thirty-one.

"I like the number," he says. "It's extremely prime. A big party to celebrate my prime and," he declares as if on a whim, "the launch of Finer Materials."

"What's that?"

"Nothing yet." He sounds happy. "I'm launching a production company." Of course he'd spoken about this before. Over the years he had come up with multiple business plans. He'd drafted up mission statements, outlined start-up costs, anticipated state and federal taxes; he'd performed minute market analyses, described sales trends and plans for distribution. "I found a way just to do it cheap. Just to start small."

"Demetri!" I say, and then I offer him other options to celebrate. We can rent a truck and go to Ikea. We can take a bachata class. We can do anything that does not place him, Nati, and me in the same room, though of course I do not say this, because of course a part of me wants it.

A MONTH LATER we're at a large house on Long Island. I can only afford the house for one night. It's near the town we grew up in, but this one is monied and less populated. When Demetri and I pull into the driveway, before the guests, we both think of our mother. The house possesses a curated asymmetry—imbricated rooflines, a jutting wrap-around porch. Inside, it's all vaulted ceilings, everything is clad in Calacatta marble. Demetri mentions our mother by name. One of the house assistants overhears him. "Marion!" she says, thinking it's a friend. "Such a pretty name." We nod at her.

People arrive in small groups until all at once it is a party. Everyone talks loud and looks in Demetri's direction, wondering if he is overhearing what they are saying—if he is finding it interesting, because of the seed it contains of a thing he once said.

I wander around. I notice a small ceramic elephant on a large golden lampstand. I pick it up and rub its belly. There are two tiny pinholes at the most distended bit of belly. I remind myself that these tiny holes are accidents—formed when gasses escape in the kiln. I feel extreme relief that this little elephant can breathe.

Soon a man I do not recognize comes up to me. A group of men is with him.

"We're all dying to see it!" this man says. His friends agree. I can tell by their kind and bland paternal faces that they mean my new project. In the month between Demetri's request for a party and the party itself, I was awarded a Burning Man art grant. I used it—the $7,000—to pay for rent as I spent time zooming in on massive, high-resolution digital photos of the world's most famous painted masterpieces. I made an analysis of the individual pixels: the precise shades of gold in the lower third portion of the *Mona Lisa*'s eye, or the exact silvered pink on the lower lip of Botticelli's Venus. Tens of millions of pixels altogether. I drafted a chart organized by hue, saturation, and value, and—at the time of the party—have just begun to go to public schools, into art classes, where children color their squares with pens designed to render the specific pigment I'll need. I then plan to place those squares together to re-form the picture, on a massive scale, all done in a child's hand. The series is to be called *Even a Child Could Do It.* Demetri thought it was conservative, backward looking, kitschy. I did not tell him it was the only idea I submitted that got me an award. I was excited because it would be put into a public library. People—including children—could touch it.

"We are all dying to see it," one of the men keeps telling me. "Even a child could do it! That's fabulous. I see the point you're making. Even if my child could not do it."

The music is loud. More people come toward us.

"Your child could color a square. But, Ava, can you talk to us more about the point? Is it to show even great geniuses all start with the primal stuff? Blocks of color? That it's all just blocks of color? What are you going for?"

"My child was part of it. She did *The Last Supper*'s table."

"Mine just got gray, probably sky."

"Ava, sky or eyelid? Gray?"

But I'm watching Nati's black braid behind them. Demetri is standing there with her. I did not see her come in. Now she is five feet in front of me. Her braid ends right at the nape of her neck. The meat of it is healthy, but the end of it frays.

It's my first time seeing them together. I notice how close they stand, side by side—their skin not touching but almost—an almost touch, an almost release. I look away. Everyone else is roaming around eating micro bites of food: Little pieces of toast topped with dollops of feta and drizzled with honey. Toothpicks pierced through stacks of fried crab. I stand by the trays and think of my mother—how once she planned a party, got scared that no one would come, hid in her bedroom as guests arrived—as I overhear Nati saying *scherzo* to Demetri.

"Scherzo," she says in her accent. "Means joke." She's smiling. She has not looked at me. "Like funny . . . like, joke. Scherzo."

Demetri cannot do accents, I want to tell them both. His *r*'s have always stayed immutably hard, like the *R*s in "ardor" or "territory."

"There's a *really* soft roll, Demetri," Nati says. She pronounces the *R* in his name with the same soft roll. *"Scherrrzo."* She takes Demi's chin in her unmanicured hand. "You can say it."

"Scherzo." Demetri is also smiling, staring at her wet,

black eyes—each lash separated, coming at you like a fragile claw. He tries again.

Nati leans back laughing, keeping her hand tight on Demetri's chin. It's the same grip I've seen her use for her purse, when lifting it to the table. Also when she pulls a comforter over a bed, when she's tight on my hips. Demi clears his throat: "Lemme tell you a funny scherzo." Nati laughs again. "I'm full of great scherzo," Demetri goes on. He is laughing from watching her.

Nati catches her breath. "*Non è uno scherzo*," she says, placing her palms on his chest.

Demetri weaves his arms around her, webs his fingers behind her back.

I realize that Nati seems to love my brother in the mistaken way all women love him, with the feeling of finally possessing something vital and good.

"That's very very very bad," Nati says to him. His arms are still webbed around her. "Very very very." English, I remind myself, lacks the inherent emphatic quality of Italian, and so she has to make it up. She's sticking her tongue out. Demetri leans in.

From behind me a voice cuts into my ear: "Ava, does this mean you've officially made it? And will you watch it?"

I twist my gaze out of Nati's braid and realize the group of men have left me. I must have answered them. Now in front of me is James, who—he is excited to tell me—has heard that there is to be a film on the life of Ava Stern. It will be small and is just being produced.

"A film?" I ask. Before I have time to consider how unlikely this is, I prepare myself for Demetri's lecture on why he should've been the one to make it. "What do you mean by film?"

"Something like a documentary," he says. He tilts his glass to finish his martini. "Very much on the down-low." He explains he only heard of it through his cousin in Echo Park, whose friend over in Westwood was interviewed. "It's all secrets and hearsay." James smiles at me. "Maybe it's not even happening."

I ask him who is making it.

"It's Liam Lesser or something," he says. He nods. The ridges in his nose—broken twice from drunken spills—contain the only angles on his face. His tic is to press on the ridges in a way where he appears to have smelled something awful. I tear his hand from his face.

"They'll think it's me," I say.

He stands on his tippy-toes to sniff my neck. "Anyway, here's hoping it's good. Or bad. Whichever benefits you." James raises his glass to cheers with me, remembers he's finished, and pulls me by my arm to the bar.

We pass Demetri on the way out the back. "Lesser," I call to him, knowing Nati will have to hear me. "Do we know a Lesser?"

Demetri hardly looks up at me. I can tell from his smile he's feeling his drink. "She thinks everyone is a lesser," he tells Nati. She shushes him, looks down.

The party wears on. "Superstition" by Stevie Wonder plays. A group of people I don't know say they're heading out onto the beach. Nati follows them. So does Demetri.

But as they begin to approach the sea, Demetri turns around. He heads back to the porch. I stand by the back door and watch him. He lifts himself onto the picnic table.

As he lifts, I notice that all of his muscle is gone. He is too lean.

"Demetri," I start to say. Once on the table he begins to dance. He stomps on the wood until it starts to splinter. He starts to sing with Stevie, tilting his neck to the sky so I can see it throttle as he belts the chorus. He pulls others up on the table to join him. I notice a desperation in his movements, an impatience or an excess in his rhythm—he is a fraction in front of the beat, singing just ahead of the lyrics. He is turning his body around so that he's not facing the ocean, which is now working up the shore—high tide.

It occurs to me, watching him, that he has not been on this beach since we left it.

I turn to look out toward the sand. Various scenes play out before me. People are drinking and talking with their hands. Eventually someone sets up a bonfire. Nati's friend steps on an ember. From afar I watch Nati's arm as she holds the friend's ankle and blows on the heel.

Others, drunk, go all the way out onto the dock, take off their clothing, and jump into the Sound.

Demetri and I do not. Instead, I begin to walk out onto the sand, and he surprises me by coming to stand with me. We watch the guests fade and reappear through water.

"We can't swim," Demi says when we're called into the waves. I feel us watching Nati. She's heading into the water. She's taken off her shirt and is letting her skirt balloon around her. The moon makes her hair bright black. I try to find her face, but it dips under too often. Feeling Demetri watch her beside me, a warm current courses down my back. Demetri, I want to tell him. He presses his toes into the sand, almost loses balance, catches himself and explodes in laughter, and suddenly the whole thing—everything, life—erupts before me as something so minimal, too long.

We wait as the swimmers grow tired. They crawl out of the water, hair slung black over their eyes. I feel Demetri reach for me, then stop himself. I leave him before Nati emerges.

The party dwindles. Then it ends. When people leave, they leave in big groups, so that when the house is finally empty it is as if entire blocks of space have been ripped off, and all that is left of the house is the kitchen, where Demetri and I stand, cleaning. The music is off.

We can't figure out the house's dishwasher, so Demetri is hand drying the plates.

"Who is this Liam Lesser?" I ask, taking a seat on one of the chrome stools.

I can't see Demetri's face when he answers: "It's a pseudonym, I think. Of that boy we knew, Levi, from high school. I think he uses a pseudonym," he repeats himself. I notice his movements turn stiff, almost suspicious, but I don't press him. "You knew him," he says. I watch as he puts a clean plate down, lifts a dirty one.

Levi. It takes me a minute to retrieve the face attached to the name—and after a moment it arrives as a big, oiled nose and a thick, unified brow. I had sketched him once, when I found him in the nurse's office for a headache. He sat nicely. Last name Landau.

"He replaced double-L initials with double-L initials?"

"He wanted it to be different."

"That's not different."

"There aren't degrees of difference, with names. A different name is an absolutely different name." Demetri's voice, its edge when turning frivolous distinctions into law.

"Do you think, Demetri, that Sophie and Sophia, Amelia and Amalia. They're so different?" As soon as I say this I realize that they are.

"Yes." He is using a rag to make concentric circles on the plate, and now holds it out in front of him, like it has been not just cleaned but encoded with a new molecular structure. I want to ask if Nati's way of saying Demetri makes his name more appealing to him. And then I want to ask about all the other ways he feels he changed through her. "Liam," Demi continues, "is different enough. Liam Lesser."

"You're right." I twirl in my stool. "That woman today liked the name Marion."

"I like it, too. It means sea of bitterness," Demetri tells me like I've forgotten. "If you remember Levi"—he can't see me, but I nod—"he became a director. Probably one of the few people who made it out alive. I mean out of our town. I know him from some of those circles. He's supposed to be pretty decent."

"Well," I say, "he's making something about us . . . or, me. Do you think we'll be in it?" I envision myself seated next to Demetri in a scene, unaware of being filmed, and I cringe.

Demetri moves on to bowls. He hasn't looked at me. He does not bring up any prior conversation. "It's nice he's thinking of us . . ."

"I can't remember if I liked Levi." This is false. I liked him well. But Demetri is being too quiet, and I need to provoke.

"You never like anyone." He lays down another bowl. "I mean you don't like Nati," he says.

I feel my ears drain of blood. Still I manage to speak. "I absolutely do not not like her. I like her. Good hair."

"How do you know what her hair's like?"

"By looking at her."

"But you don't," he says.

"I don't what?"

"You don't look at her." He doesn't know. I hold my breath. "And she notices. She knows that you who looks at everything—you who has to stop moving and are fucking obnoxious as you make me wait—you do not look at her."

"Does she say this?"

"No. She wouldn't tell me that. But I can tell it bothers her that you don't."

"It bothers her that I don't look at her?"

"Yes," he says.

"Well."

Demetri turns to watch me.

"Well, I don't need to look at her." I think of what would sound natural. "I see her when I close my eyes."

"That doesn't count," says Demi. But he's smiling. "Also that's really fucking weird."

I think of how far I can take his innocence. "How could I like someone that you've convinced to be against me?"

"What do you mean I've convinced her against you!" He's laughing.

"I hear what you say about me." Although I'm laughing, and so is he.

"I say nothing about you. She has no opinions of you!" He turns to me.

"Then why would she care what I think!"

We are silent. Then the cold clap of ceramic as Demetri stacks more bowls.

"You never talk to me about her," I say at last. He doesn't answer. "You don't talk to me much at all. Actually about anything." I have a flash of his hunched form pacing out on the street.

"I don't need to talk to you," he says. "I hear you at all times. I hear you when I pray for silence."

"You never pray," I say. "Do you think they asked Nati for an interview, for whatever Lorne is making?"

"It's Liam. And no."

"Why?"

"She hardly knows me," Demetri says. This is intended to surprise me, and it does.

I stay very cool. "I thought it's been some time? A half year?"

"Yes. But it takes about three years to really, really know someone."

"Is that science?"

"Yes," he says, taking on his tone, but playing it up. "It takes three years to know someone in a stable way. Biochemicals. It takes three years for those chemicals to stabilize around a certain person. Unless you're in an extremely healthy relationship. Then the chemicals never stabilize. And you are free to continue to misunderstand each other in a way that's good for both of you."

"You're making this up."

"I'm not," he says. "In a healthy relationship there is room left for the other person. That's how fossils survived for billions of years under the earth. They could breathe in the mud and clay and were not compressed into fucking particles."

"Demetri"—I am still twirling on my stool—"sometimes people don't want the breathing room. Sometimes people want to be smothered and demolished. To get it all over with."

He ignores me. "If I had this"—Demetri holds up a miniature dehydrator—"I would make apricots and mince them, and put them in salads, and into yogurt, homemade ice cream." He begins slapping his hands against his thighs. "I'd put them in scones, in pies, in pasta. On cheese, on ham . . ."

I remember Nati brought a big pastry box to the house. As Demetri keeps listing foods, I get off my stool and walk across the kitchen. The door to the fridge is heavy and the cold air makes me blink hard. The shelves are empty but for two cartons of milk, a glass bottle of cream, and a plain white box. Inside the box I find a large, untouched carrot cake, with chopped walnuts spackled along the side. Iced across the cake is an orange carrot and, in cursive, *DEMETRI*.

I bring the cake over to my stool and take a fork to the first *E* of Demetri. "Dmetri," I say in my Russian accent.

"If you spelled it that way, you'd be a criminal." I lick icing off the tines. Demetri tells me he is a criminal. One of those kinds where the crimes are so heinous that they don't actually exist because people can't fathom their horror. The brain can't accommodate them. They are biochemically incomputable.

"Why commit them?" I ask him.

He only holds a butter knife to his neck.

I don't know what prompts me to say it, but for some reason I'm telling him, as I fork more letters off his name, that Italians don't have the letter *K*, or *J*.

"You're right," is all he says. He is finishing cleaning the forks, one tine at a time. "You are right."

"Thank you." I yawn.

"Exhausting for you?"

"Yes." I put my head on the island. Its granite is cool against my ear. The quiet kitchen feels like youth, when countertops collect all your bones and time, and no one is waiting for you.

I turn once more in my stool, and for a number of minutes Demetri and I are silent.

"Bring me the carrot," he says. He is done cleaning and is leaning against the edge of the sink. "I need a vegetable."

I take the butcher knife and dig it slantwise into the icing, using my finger to help the whole slab onto the blade. I bring the blade to Demetri.

"Enjoy."

He makes a streak through the carrot with his fork. "Sugary," he says. "They should make them all this way."

I notice he is more exhausted than I am—slick grooves have formed around his eyes. I've never seen them before. He's aging, I think. We're aging. I pretend—even to myself—to realize for the first time how odd it is that Nati has gone home.

"Are you feeling okay?"

"How do you mean?"

"Like your head?"

"Like do I know this isn't an actual carrot?" He is taking the tiniest bits of icing at a time, lifting them in little flames off his blade. "I was between carrot and radish. It's got too much red dye." He is still for a minute before he hands me a fork and nods at me to eat. "Yes, my head hurts," he continues. He wants to say more, but then is silent. I put my fork down to tell him I'm done. "No, no, no." He hands it back to me. "Demolish."

By the time we finish the carrot, and then one full slice, and then another full slice, Demetri is half asleep, leaning against the dishwasher. He pours himself a glass of water, and then pauses.

"Drink," I say.

The clock says it is just past two in the morning—late, but not that late. Demetri's hand cannot hold the glass.*

**Glass*, acrylic on canvas, extra small

"I can't hold these," he says.

"It's one glass, Demi."

He puts it down, overstudies it.

"Okay, come." I bring him to his room. His arm is too light around my neck.

"Tired," he keeps saying. And then, at his door, "I'm running a bath."

I leave him there and return to the kitchen, to the sink. There is still a bit of icing on the blade. I run the faucet until the water steams, put the knife under the faucet, and watch the remainder dissolve.

TWO DAYS LATER I take Demetri to the ER because he can't see from a migraine. This has never happened to him before. Nati is visiting Italy, and I don't ask if he'd rather have called her.

The ER is slammed. A nurse walks toward us with a soft, glacial apathy.

"Yeah. Okay. And you feel better when you're in the tub, with the lights off and a cool compress over your head?" the nurse asks him. She holds a clipboard and a pen but is not writing anything down.

"Definitely," Demetri says. His eyes have smalled into

Glass (cont.): Imagine a whiskey glass rattling. I tried to capture the blur of the objects *behind* the glass—visible because of the glass's translucence—and also the blur of the glass itself. Difficult.

raisins, even the blue has turned brown. He is sweating and pale. The freckles down his arm look desaturated,* pale flecks of dust. "But it also feels like stones are being kneaded into my eyes, so I came here." This announcement takes all his energy. "And this is my sister," he says, sitting back down.

"Hi."

The nurse pulls me aside and tells me that they don't really deal with migraines on-site at the hospital. Demetri should go home and schedule an appointment with his physician, who can refer him to a specialist.

"That he is suddenly blind and immobile does not qualify as an emergency?" I'm trying to stand with that commanding tilt in my hips. (How often I still try to move like Nati is watching me. Like she might see the arch in my lower back as I bend to reach for an apple in the supermarket, like she might see my arm flex as I lift a chair.)

"Not if we can pretty generally diagnose the cause. I can assure you that this happens all the time."

"I thought men didn't usually get migraines."

"They don't."

"But it happens all the time?"

"With men it's usually to do with testosterone." Another patient calls for her. She holds up her finger to him.

**Desaturated*, oil on linen, medium
Sometimes things work out.

"Maybe his physician can have blood work done. We just don't do that here." She gestures around to show me the existence of other people.

The man calls out again.

"But you can give him chlorpromazine," I say. I've looked it up before arriving. "Or valproic acid, for his headache."

She lifts her brow and pen at the same time, both pointing at me. "If either of you feel like waiting for six hours for an available slot, yes, we can do that. Chances are his symptoms wane before then."

I look at the man calling her and see he is bleeding through a bandage on his thigh. A child is pulling at his sleeve, jumping up and down, yelling, "Skin, Daddy! Skin, Daddy! Skin!" The man begins to moan. I think of how Nati would go talk to the child. She would lift him. She would not comfort him and tell him his father would be okay but rather she would explain the proper code of conduct in an emergency. That one is not to exceed a certain volume despite one's excruciating pain or desire for attention. She would look at him with stern, coercive eyes.

I look at Demetri, who has his eyes closed. (Two hours earlier he had called me from the bathtub. Now he's sitting in the waiting room chair, a black plastic cantilever. He's wearing a green silk robe that's dotted with little lizards and small bottles of tequila. When he called me I had been painting, so I'm there in my smock, splattered and unbrushed.

Probably looking like I should be wielding a cleaver.) I look again at the moaning man, who is too in touch with pain to feel his child at his shirt.

"Okay," I say, turning to the nurse. She is already gone.

In the cab home Demetri keeps his eyes closed. He can hardly speak.

"Low T," he says, out of nowhere. "Low testosterone." I didn't realize he'd heard us. "Jesus Christ. There's only one treatment for that. Do you know what it is?"

I say no.

He closes his eyes.

ONE WEEK LATER Demetri is scheduled to introduce a pair of young filmmakers at a Film Forum panel. He'd been using my art recently to theorize on analogous trends in modern film, and one of his essays (I did not read them) caught the directors' attention. Demetri gets all spunked up. And then, the day before the panel, he calls me. He does not know I am happily painting Nati out of me. If I can't make anything else, I might as well continue making her. His headaches have subsided, he tells me. "But low testosterone," he says. I feel him worrying around his apartment. Nati is still in Italy—a two-week trip, Demetri tells me—but nevertheless I imagine her in the corner, watching him fret. "So, low manliness. Low musk, low pheromones. Low virility. I probably can't have children. Low testosterone. Low virility. Who knew. What else does it mean? Look it up. Hot flashes, fragile bones. A dumpling dick. Hair loss. I have none of it, so far, but it's coming. A massive woman is going to branch out of me. I can hear her, this rushing in my ears. She's the ache in my head. Her nails are scratching at the backs of my eyes. I've said that already. I've been getting dumber. I've already gained five pounds." One sharp breath. "Don't come over. It's just that it's funny, the low T has revved up my libido. Now it's like I'm trying to prove it wrong." I try not to think of their bodies together. "The truth is that I don't even need or want high T, like a buffed-up lothario. Regular T would be fine. Just not low. Not low." He goes on like this, his panic working itself into circles. "Do you think you have more than me?"

The next day—the morning of the panel—Demetri wakes up unable to see. He calls me. "Not double vision, but blind," he says. "Black squares." I ask about the speech. "Nati got in this morning. She can go instead. Just have her read it. They don't care who. Can you please tell her?" he says.

It's 10:00 a.m. I take a shot of vodka with my espresso before I call her.

My whole body slips down into my groin, and I wonder how I will speak. I decide the faster the better.

"Hi," I say.

Because Demetri is involved, Nati's voice on the phone

is calm. I speak to her quickly. I tell her that Demetri is ill again and that she'll have to give the speech herself.

"Not a problem at all. It's no problem. Where's Demetri?"

"He's at his home. Are you not living together?"

She ignores me. "Is he lying down?"

"It's likely."

"Very good." I feel dead energy morph into a certain kind of excitement. I don't know why. A part of me believes she'll admit to some profundity about me, about us, that I didn't know I had attached myself to. I want her to declare she wants me again, which disturbs me.

"It is," is all I can say.

"I didn't write it to you. He has had a lot of aches recently," she says. She wants to say more. "He fell off his stool, at coffee."

"When?" I try to imagine it, the two of them sitting outside, Demetri's fall, Nati's pristine shock—her watching herself tend to him in the nearest reflective surface.

"The morning I left for Italy. He fell right off. I thought it was an attack."

"An attack?"

"I don't know the word. In Italian it's *attacco*. But not an attack like you think."

"Seizure."

"Yes. My mother, she had bad aches, too. And attacks. But hers were from deeabetts."

"From?"

"Deeabetts. Low sugar. Maybe he needs an apple." The thought of Demetri eating an apple, the crunch sending a compressive shot through his brain . . . But I say nothing. "And are you okay?" she asks quickly.

"Yes."

We take a moment. Her breath through the phone warms my ear.

"Ava," she says.

"Yes."

We wait. Because I am incorrigible, I again have the simple desire for her to tell me she misses me very much.

"Well, that's very good," she says. She starts to say more.

I break in. "I'll tell him you are all good to go."

"Yes. I'm all good to go." The idiom sounds absurdly American in her accent, like she's saying the pledge of allegiance. I think of, if we were standing together outside, how her eyes would look at me in that moment—their seriousness.

"Thank you again," I start to say. But she's already hung up. When I call Demetri to confirm, the line is busy.

That same day, his headache not abating, Demetri falls when getting out of the tub, and then vomits on himself. The next week we go to see a specialist, and a day and a half later we learn Demetri has a seraphic Greek woman unfolding inside his brain. A sphenoid wing meningioma.

A malignant brain tumor, adhering to the optic nerve and encasing* the carotid artery.

The doctor we find is Iranian. He has this immaculate, old-fashioned beauty. A thick head of gray hair and dark green eyes. When Demetri, tearless and calm, asks the doctor how serious it all is, the doctor crosses his arms. Or that's what I imagine. I am made to listen through the door because Demetri can't trust my reactions.

FOR AN ENTIRE WEEK Demetri does not answer his phone or allow me to see him.

WHEN NATI KNOCKS on my door I am not surprised. She looks undone, pale in a long leather jacket. I've never seen her eyes so black, with gray rings around them. She has come to tell me that she cannot move. She begins to say more but then is silent. I lead her into my kitchen. I expect her to resist but she stays close to me. I hope to smell Demetri on her, but I do not. We stand together, saying nothing. I bring out a blanket and offer her Demetri's spot on the

---

**Encasing*, watercolor on rice paper, medium
In my dream scenario a doctor comes to the show and looks at this painting and says to himself that this is an image of a malignant brain tumor that adheres to the optic nerve and encases the carotid artery. In my other dream scenario a child comes to the show and thinks it's heaven.

floor. Not that she knows it's his. She takes my offer. "I can't stay," she says. But soon she falls asleep. I sit and sketch her in quick strokes of charcoal. The binder in my graphite stick is weak, and on the page she nearly crumbles.

IN THIS PERIOD I have no introspection. I am unconscious. Two weeks later, Demetri lets me in. The tumor is serious, but he is not. I come over and let him show me survival rates, even though I know them by heart—for every hundred people, thirty dead. We sit together and watch videos of neurosurgeries. Doctor after doctor, masked and gloved, addressing the camera with the casual energy of a "Get Ready with Me!" vlog. Suddenly Demetri claps once. "Okay, y'all!" He's talking to an imagined medical crew. "So, today I prefer a nine-blader for the vascular," he says. He turns to me and smiles. "Goddamn. Like carving swine." He touches his head.

BUT HIS PRESENCE is unreliable. When he doesn't answer his phone for three days, I call Nati. No answer. Finally, I go to his apartment and all of the lights are off. I don't see him at first. It's because he is silhouetted by the sun, which whittles his skin to vapor. I had expected the apartment to smell. I expected piled dishes, the scent of prolonged sleep and unwashed clothing, unflushed toilet; I expected urine in stickered circles on the seat. But everything is sterilized. It smells like bleach.

"Demetri," I say.

When he looks up at me—his face alive, dark, and hard—I pretend I can speak.

"That's true," he says, responding to something I can't remember saying.

The possibility of Demetri dying has no relationship to reality. His death is alien—I'm aware of its potential presence but am uninvested and unbelieving in its course.

Still, I have to entertain him. "Have you thought about your afterlife body?"

"No. I'd like to crawl right back into this one," Demetri says. His voice is low, coming up from some deep well. "Into this body. Although maybe I flatline briefly. I could enjoy that." He looks up into the ceiling. "I want to be in a small, fat, and fluffy body. A duck." He looks up on top of his mantel. "But yes eventually, I'd like to get back into this one. My idiot body. You know that I'm hosting a cellular civil war. I am a desecrated country." He looks at me so meaningfully that I laugh. "I'm Belchite in Spain." I have no idea what this means. "I'm a breathing memorial site." At first I think he means for our mother. "Memorializing my fucking self."

I want to ask him how he is feeling in a more general sense. How long he's been sitting there, or how he managed to lose so much weight in so little time. Tell me your secret, I'd put on my Valley girl voice. But we're silent.

In that little room time begins to pass without us. It takes on texture until Demetri breaks it—he says he's been thinking about nothing new at all. How depressing it is that death—dying—has not made him a more complicated person, how it has not complicated his thinking. He's still thinking, for example, about petrified wood, and how it might look as a backsplash in the kitchen. And about smart-home technology, which he wants to install so he can clap off his lights and close his blinds and turn music on and off. He's been thinking—as he lies there dying—how he's becoming more dependent on the technology people have when they feel they're really living, what people acquire to show they've really made it. That they're full-on in life. "And blah, blah, blah, Ava. It's funny, all of it now seems in preparation for death. Socrates said philosophy was preparation for death. But technology is the true preparation. Our advancements are just new ways to stay still. They are our desire for complete, eternal immobility. We're all trying to die while we're alive so that death itself will be less momentous. We're so scared." He tells me that even all his big questions are old, questions about our mother and father, and if he and our father were right, and we killed her.

"We had nothing to do with it," I tell him. But I know his answer.

"We saw the light turn on outside." Demetri and I

shared a room—the only room where the window looked onto the porch, which led directly to the Sound. "We saw it turn on and we did not call for her."

"We were sleeping," I say.

"We weren't. I wasn't."

"We couldn't be sure it was her." I sit up now.

"We knew that it was her."

"She always came back inside," I say. Sometimes our mother went out late. She'd water her philodendrons.

"We should have known that at one point she wouldn't," Demetri says.

"We couldn't have known that."

"I could have known it," he says.

"You did not know it."

He doesn't speak.

"Not saving someone is not the same thing as killing them," I say.

Then we are silent. Demetri had told us to stay in our room. It was late. Our father was asleep on the opposite side of the house.

But Demetri had seen the floodlight switch on, and it was he who said not to go out and check. I had even sat up, ready to go to her. From his own bed he shook his head no.* He and my mother had spent the day together. He was tired.

**No*, acrylic on canvas, extra small

When we woke the next day, the sun was too high. No one had gotten us up. Our mother had already been found, her body pushed against a stack of eroded rock. Our father had left in the morning for the police and had not returned.

"You are trying to have some kind of revelation, Demetri."

"I know."

"Why?"

"I have to. I only have time for a few more. One of them has to change me. I can't just die as myself." He stares at me until I look away. *A lot of people walk around*, I want to say, but then I can't remember the rest—lyrics to a song he showed me years ago, by a band I can't remember—*with grave sites in their mind*. But that's not it.

I wish I could remember.

He looks at me, as if suddenly bewildered by the life that never happened to him.

I say: "We know what did it." I cross and recross my legs. "I mean I know who."

I expect Demetri to launch into a defense, for him to explain that our father only bought the camera to protect himself and so that he and our mother could play. But instead, Demetri nods. Because it is not something we would

---

No (cont.): Degas and Toulouse-Lautrec and all those guys have their way of bleeding ballerina tutus together. In this I have tried to bleed hair together with the same kind of energetic sway, like there's muscle beneath the hair kicking it all together this way and that.

say out loud, not something we could explain, only a distinct impression, announced in us at all times, that our mother would not have killed herself had she not been able to film it.

Demetri's eyes land on the table between us. He holds his gaze there. And then, just as he seems to focus, he falls asleep, right there on the couch. I nod off on the chair.

I wake up to his voice. In the darkness, he doesn't realize I myself have fallen asleep. "Mostly, though, I'm feeling relieved," he is saying. I can see through a kind of inverted lighting that he is giving me the tucked-under look. "Even though you didn't congratulate me."

"For?" I had not checked my mail, the news, anything, since his diagnosis. I think he is going to tell me he is up for an award. That he has won a grant. That he's been accepted into some experimental trial. That he's on the cusp of living.

"All I had was this thing"—he points to his head—"and not a diminishing cock . . . and now I won't even get to live long enough."

"To really diminish."

"—properly. Naturally." He puts his neck back.* "Shit."

**Neck back*, oil on linen, extra small
Stand facing someone. Put your hand on their forehead. Push their head back so that their neck is exposed. Find it here.

NATI COMES OVER AGAIN. This time she's frantic.

"And he's telling me he does not want me to see him because he is forgetting things, and then what if he forgets me, and I mean that he is blacking out, is what he's saying to me." Her sentences overlap one another. She's both hushed and histrionic. The red rimming her eyes makes them look almost symmetric. I wonder how aware she is of her perfect expression of grief, and why I feel such cruelty toward her when I sense she means what she says, as if she has no right to meaning.

I do sense that it's the time to ask her about Demetri and why she is committed to him. She can't deny the question now. She'll feel—I tell myself—that it's the last time she'll be asked.

"Why do I desire him?" She's pacing.

"Yes."

"I can't answer that, Ava. You want to embarrass me."

"I don't."

She walks toward me, or rather her knees drive her forward. "Yes. Because you want to feel the most of everything. You need to feel the most for him. You need to feel the most for everyone and everything. God forbid you are outfelt. Or I love Demetri for reasons that are not true for you and are therefore not credible to you." I watch her knuckles. "And then to deal with your superior feeling. I'd believe in it. I'd believe you. I'd believe that you felt more than me. And that makes me hate myself. You are extremely dominating." As she's talking, I have the image of Demetri, a child, clapping at a community puppet show, how I thought he was rising to give what looked like a standing ovation to the puppets, until I realized he was clapping up at a bird that was tottering along a fence, screaming at it to come down off the fence, that it didn't have to do it, it didn't have to do it, laughing to himself in a way that makes me—standing across from Nati—laugh out loud. She hears this and mistakes it, maybe, for mockery. "I will believe that you are right and that I am not feeling correctly or not profoundly, or not as much as I should, not as much as you. And so I can't discuss things with you, Ava."

"I thought," I say, "that you could not bring it up to me because you wanted me to think you still, maybe, wanted me. I hoped that maybe it would pain you."

"That what would pain me?"

"That it would pain you to tell me why you love someone else—if you did, or do still, also, want me."

"You were being so good to yourself?"

I feel my neck reddening. "I think so."

"Well, it can be both things, no?" She turns to me.

I tell her I don't know what this means.

She turns away again. "I can't talk about him."

"Why?" I hear the edge in my voice.

She doesn't speak. I stand there and enjoy the backs of her knees as she paces. I watch her hips.

"His shame excites me," she says. "I like to apologize for him. I like to run up to people and say sorry for him. That sounds so bad. It's not. I can't explain . . ." Her voice—her accent—makes her sound like she is tilting off something. "He gave out the wrong directions. He couldn't say sorry to the family. I went up and I gave the right directions and I apologized for him. Demetri stood behind me and just waved. He does, he has a Grecian sense of shame. But it's good to have that. Everyone else is a savage." She pauses. "He cannot merge onto a highway. We take the curve, get onto the ramp—"

"Where were you going?"

She ignores me. "It's time to merge and he stops. Everyone behind us is honk, honk, honk. We sit for ten minutes. He's breathing deep, preparing himself. Then he just closes his eyes and slams on the pedal. Like life is nothing after all. Meanwhile I'm dying, but we are laughing . . ."

"Okay," I say. We stand for a minute. I watch her feet.

Out my window we hear the traffic. It's windy and the glass is creaking. Nati's hands are dry. The veins in her wrist rise softly out of her skin and I want to run my finger over them. We stand awhile longer.

"Do you want to see them?" I ask her. My portraits of

her are in the next room. There are nine of them. I need her to take one, for her to do what she will with it, so that I can explode and move beyond her. "See them. Take one," I say.

"No." She doesn't look at me.

"They're right in there. You're in there." I point to my studio, the large closet.

She's never been inside it and has only seen the portraits in progress, in glances, as I paint them.

She doesn't move. But when I turn to walk toward my studio door, I know she's following me. I open the door. I want her to see the clutter, to smell the stench of the little room: chemical citrus and rubber, the smell of damp cotton. I feel her standing behind me, now in full sight of my portraits. I step to the side and tell her to go forward.

"Look," I say.

She waits, and then walks into the room so that she's in the center of it. First she looks left. There are my three acrylics. Her body painted in bright, high-voltage pigments. Orange, yellow, blue, green. In each of these she's leaning against the wall, her ligaments pulling, her arms raised, her legs lifting her onto her tippy-toes, her hair flipped thick to one side. Nati observes them and is mute.

She steps toward the next three. I've painted her on tissue paper. My brush is small here. She's in watercolor, with the plums and saffrons blended. The undertones of soil. In each of these she's sitting on the floor. Her legs are crossed. Her toes peek out under her knees. In one she's leaning toward me, hungry, animal, and delicate at once, with her breasts hanging shallow. In another she's leaning back on her palms, her eyes closed, her neck networked with strokes of purple and brown.

Finally she steps in front of the last three. She's in sweet-leaf and willow greens. She's wet in mints and clovers. Impastoed. I've loaded my palette knife with oil. I'd made quick sweeping strokes of her body sprawled across the floor. Her limbs look spliced together. Her ribs break out of her skin as she lies contorted, leaning back on her fore-arms. Breath fills her stomach. She's heaving, or writhing, or exulting.

In the room I stand behind her, watching her observe herself.

She's not going to be able to look at me, I know it.

Minutes pass. To see her standing among herself over-whelms me.

She steps backward.

I wait to see what she'll say.

She doesn't move. I wait so long that my knee begins to ache. I haven't been sleeping. And then I wait so long that I sit down and, finding the floor softer than usual, close my eyes. I close them first only in intervals. Then for an extended period of time.

The emptiness of the room wakes me. I stand up, knowing she has left. There's an ache in my lower back, and as I stretch I stare into Nati on the canvas directly across from me, the space between her ribs, and then her chest, her neck. I convince myself that my depictions exceed her.

That I like them more than her.

That maybe Demetri would, too, and that after all maybe the whole small point was to create for us an über-object, an überimage.

I think this until I leave the room and enter my kitchen and find her there, undressing, placing her palms against the counter. "Okay," she says. "You can do it again."

I don't pretend to consider. I take out my paints. I think of Demetri and begin to shake. Nati stays perfectly still.

NOW DEMETRI IS BALDING and forgetting and a show-off—because in this state he wants to go to Italy. He is six months into his illness. Some days I think he will die. The next I am sure he will harness his remaining energy and discover something: a concept, an undiscovered angle through a lens. I want to ask him why Italy—which we've been to—but I know it's because Nati is there, again, visiting her dying mother. He doesn't know that I know this. ("I have no choice," she told me in a violent whisper on the phone.) I encourage Demetri's trip. The doctors demand a good reason for us to go, and I find one by offering to speak at the Rome University of Fine Arts. Months ago Nati had helped me place three of my shampoo paintings there, and so I convince them that I owe them a talk. The doctors warn Demetri that the flight might exacerbate his symptoms: headaches, dizziness, unpredictable behavior. They say they cannot legally keep him in the States—but if they could . . .

We arrive alive, Demetri even more so than me. On the night before my lecture we go to the discoteca and it's crowded.

Demetri heads right for the dance floor. I sit and observe his body rocking side to side, his feet hitting the downbeat. On the crowded floor, he is alone with his eyes closed, looking ill and ecstatic. A bass drum kicks up his body, throbbing at his temples.

The women take turns staring. My brother: a sick-thin, hulking man who—when he shakes his head to the beat—releases stray strands of hair that float* off his body in microscopic quivers of light. Demi and I don't know anyone in the room. They are all Italians. Tanner than us, warmer in the eyes, caramel haired. They don't dance like Americans. They dance the way Nati dances, to sweat. I have already exhausted myself. Demetri has not. He is pumping

---

*Float, oil on linen, extra small
The little floating hairs are not painted with a paintbrush, but rather with the sharp edge of a tiny plastic toothpick, whose other end is shaped like a cow. It was one of those toothpicks that they stick in a steak. I found it at the back of my silverware drawer, along with a mostly melted candle and a half-used ball of twine. The candle—I'm remembering—is from Demetri's thirtieth birthday. The twine is for turkey bondage.

his legs, trying hard to forget his own body with so much success that he grows numb and falls down.

I stand up to go to him. But a woman beats me there. She's small. Not pretty head-on but very attractive in profile. She touches his arm and helps him up. She says something he doesn't understand. I hear her laughter when she realizes he is an American. It sounds the way all foreign laughter sounds—kind, mocking. I can't see his face but I know he must be smiling, his teeth implying all kinds of earnest American questions and jokes without his asking or telling any of them. He's looking down her shirt thinking of Nati but is also thinking: I am going to die.

And so the woman, whose dress is loose around her waist and hips but tight around her breasts, laughs again, throws her hair behind her back, and in one swift movement bends down to her knees. She stays down there, squatting, swaying. Demetri looks down at her spine. I can't quite tell what she's doing. She's crouched beneath him, so I imagine she must be gazing up at the shadow of his jaw, at the concavity where his stomach used to be.

In one liquid movement the woman gets up onto her tippy-toes and whispers something in his ear. His hips begin to move with hers. He stays high on the balls of his feet. The woman leads him, and he moves as she moves, tilting his body with such precision that he gets it wrong.

In a break between songs, the woman pushes herself

away from him and walks toward the bathroom. Demetri stands for a moment. Then he spreads his fingers out wide and moves each finger to the beat, turns his head, and finds me. He comes over with his face silver with sweat, his hair knotted across his forehead.

He collapses in the chair I've pulled out. "She couldn't tell," he says. As he sits I catch a glimpse of his profile, a gray cut of jaw.

"Couldn't tell what?" We have to shout over the music.

"Couldn't tell about my cancer."

I nod. "Or that's why she danced with you." I'm shouting. "She sought it out. Not out of pity but grace. This is a religious country, Demi."

He nods. "Or she smelled a foreigner. She smelled America."

"Your other cancer."

"At one point, you know, it wasn't cool to hate your country." He closes his eyes.

"I don't hate my country." We are still screaming.

"Just some people in it," he says.

We argue about something.

"Yes. But a country comes down to its people," I say at one point.

Eventually Demetri pauses and then screams back at me: "I actually have no idea what we're talking about." He's trying to laugh. "Tired," he says. He is in permanently bad lighting. He slips off his shoes, arches his back, lifts his ankles, and places his feet on my lap. "Can you," he says. He means rub them.

"No."

"You have to."

"Why?"

"Because I have cancer."

"Not of the foot."

"No, but it's in my *blood*. And there's blood in my feet. I have cancer of the feet."

"All men are mortalling me," I yell.

The weight of his ankles on my lap. "Funny," he says, "because tonight I feel immortal. Did you watch me before?" I look from the dance floor back to his face. "I was dancing. Lifting my hands over my head and moving. And I saw this man, he was moving in kind of the same way as me."

"Really?"

"Yeah. With his hands over his head and his neck kind of tilted back, and he looked like he wanted to dance with me. So I said, why not? And I moved closer to him, and he moved closer to me. And I kept thinking, I guess I'm going to do this. I guess I'm going to dance with him. This is life. This is life. He's alive and I'm alive. And then, at the last moment, I realized it was the mirror, and that I'd been dancing toward myself. And then I just laughed so hard I fell down. And that's when she, the woman, came and found me. But I was still laughing too hard to dance. So she kind of held me. And then once I composed myself, we danced. But I still feel, you know, that I missed out on the man." When he laughs his smile reflects the disco, the colors dulled* across his mouth.

In the morning Demetri is too sick to go to my event. He can't get up to use the restroom. I call the university to cancel. We fly home.

"NO ONE IN MY STATE has to explain anything," Demetri tells me. He had kept everyone locked out for two weeks, and then finally invited me over. "Everything should be being explained to me," he says. The doctors have told him it is best for him to move permanently into his apartment, for comfort. "For comfort!" he yells.

He tells me, when I ask, that he is having happy dreams.

"They are serene," he says.

"I've been having nightmares," I say. "Do you want me to tell you them?"

"No."

He falls asleep and I roam around. In the kitchen Nati's name is a whisper among the nurses as they change shifts. She and I silently coordinate it so that we are never around

---

**Dulled*, acrylic on canvas, extra small
Try to picture what the moon would look like if the sun were many neon colors.

Demetri at the same time. When she comes to my apartment everything we do, we do in silence. At Demetri's I overhear the nurses talking:

"Nati was here earlier."

"Nati will be coming later."

"Nati dropped it off already."

Nati has been studiously going about administrative duties that I credit to her on a delay: A plush new red carpet, layered on top of the old red carpet, arrives on the floor of Demetri's sickroom, and I think one of the nurses has put it there by accident—I sleep on it nonetheless. Letters addressed to me appear on Demetri's table. I think I myself have brought them to my own attention. When there is a prepared dinner in the fridge, I think I must be eating someone else's meal. I am generous with the credit I allow myself.

When I sense Demetri is in a deep sleep, I say goodbye to the nurses and take my leave.

TWO DAYS LATER Nati calls me. That day Demetri has again decided not to answer anyone. His door is locked. He wants to die alone, like a princess. I'm home and pacing when she calls. She starts by saying she has to tell me something. We're disconnected. She's the one who calls back. "Nati," I say.

"Did you talk today?" she asks.

"He hasn't seen me," I say. "He hasn't answered my calls."

"No?"

"No."

"I'm worried it's now the end," she says. "And it's my fault. Last night." She pauses. "I was so happy to see him. I might have been dramatic. I can't remember. I drank. I wanted to make love. I was wearing my good things. And he was very unable, Ava. And this whole time he's been able, and last night he was finally absolutely unable. He was unable. And he laughed, at first, he said you predicted it."

I begin to protest.

"He was joking," she interrupts me, "and then he became stressed. Or distressed. I mean worse than distressed, you know. He reddened. Then all the blood left him and he became so white. I can only say his name so many times, Ava. When he kicked me out, I decided, okay, I will leave. He will get better when I leave, and so I left. And now no answer."

"No answer to me, either."

"Are you listening to what I'm saying to you?"

"Yes!"

We wait.

"People are interested in his new production house," she tells me. Demetri had not spoken to me about it. "People want to send him their ideas."

"He shouldn't take them," I say.

"No?"

"No. He has so many of his own."

"Of his own ideas?" Nati's voice lifts.

"Yes. That he can produce."

"Ava, he is dying."

"I know."

By her breath, I know she's about to be righteous: "But I can't tell if you're really thinking of it?" I would tell her that I have no time to think about it because I am too busy standing for hours, feeling the callusing of my softest places, feeling my mouth open and simply stay open, the idiocy borne of grief; that if I've not been thinking about it it's because I've been thinking of nothing. But she goes on, her voice too soft now to really be gentle: "Or you're not thinking of it because you're creating it? Are you painting his death or something?" I don't answer. "I mean, don't you make everything about him? Your portraits of me—are they not about him?"

"Nati."

"Maybe I am a very brilliant person. Maybe I do know all about certain passions. Maybe I wanted to pose for you—just to see what you'd make of Demetri's want. Maybe I wanted to get closer to him and only to him. I mean from the very beginning. From the start. Maybe a lot of myself takes place offstage, without you. Maybe you even worried about that. Maybe I think a lot of things and maybe that's why I haven't really helped you. I haven't given you permanence—maybe I could have and I didn't. Maybe you wondered why I didn't."

"No," I lie to her, "I never once wondered that." I wait for her to end our call. She doesn't.

And then I hear the way she says heartbeat. "Because there was a heartbeat, and I had found it that day, I mean just yesterday. Or the doctor found it. And I was excited to tell him. I didn't know when to tell him. I didn't even know whether to tell him at all. I got drunk. Not responsible. But it was just once."

"A heartbeat where?"

"What do you mean where?"

"A child?" I hear myself ask. I feel myself not knowing and knowing still.

"Ava," Nati says. "You have no respect for my confusion . . ." She waits. I don't breathe. "I'm not saying it right. You know your language is horrible. Dead." She means English. She's going to break. I tell her she is wrong. I pause once more. When I next speak Nati listens with patience. I agree with her—that she should not tell Demetri—and tell her that instead she needs to take care of things. I do not use the word terminate.

"Okay," she says, to affirm she is listening.

I explain there is not a way for Demetri's child to exist without him, and that his fear of fatherhood would expand in death. "If you tell him now he will be in fear. And then he would die afraid. And we—I mean Demetri and I—have seen how that goes." I wait for her to respond, for her to indicate she knows all about our father. She says nothing. "And I do not want that for him. It is an impossibility." In some outer chamber of my mind my father's face bombards me. I think I sense Nati nodding. I hear a mug on her counter. I imagine steam from tea casting a sheen over her skin.

She tells me she understands me. That she is already so tired. I want to tell her how, historically, exhaustion flatters her beauty. I don't. And she does not outright agree to anything I've said. I ask her if she has any religious aversion to ending her pregnancy. I know she's shaking her head.

"But I know *you* hate the Church," she says.

"I know nothing about the Church." I say this without even thinking.

"Yes, you do, Ava," she says. She's angry. "Christ. You're always erasing yourself. Everything you know. It's you who doesn't want to exist. Why? You are afraid people will think that you're acting." She's louder. "You think everyone's going to think you're just acting. Demetri is right. You cannot commit yourself to anything. You think it's embarrassing. You're afraid no one will believe it. Because you don't believe it! You don't believe you're even existing. You don't know anything about the Church. Really? I think you hate it anyway."

"Well not as much as I know I could."

"And what else?" She's breathing heavily. "Can you please say something else? You don't say anything." I sense it's a bad time to tell her she finally seems very real to me. That this was the moment I was afraid of. "I know it because I saw it. Your paintings have an intelligence. That's true. It's lucky for you. They know things you yourself don't know. It is your curse. You are outside your own knowledge. You are empty. You fool people because what you produce is sometimes whole. You yourself are without it."

"Without what?"

"Wholeness. Anything."

"Okay."

"Everyone's waiting for you to do something big, real, and you won't. I can't say it right . . ."

"I know." I'm calm. I know it's infuriating her. I wait. "But you should be glad," I say, "that I could teach you to see these ways. That I gave you a vocabulary."

I hear her breathe. "Nasty," she says.

For a minute we break clean.

"Nati, let me ask you—if Demetri were not going through this, what would have happened? You'd have stayed with him for all time?" She doesn't answer. "Would you have come over again? Made me paint you again? You need me for something, no? Want to tell me why?" I ask her. I remind her she's yet to take a piece for her gallery. That was the basis of our entire relationship—and yet she did not take one. The one transaction she could not complete. Why? "You could have any one of them. You've never taken one. Instead you've just come back and back for more." I can sense her thought developing. "Tell me," I say. "You like it when I look at you? You like the way I see you? You want me to keep making you?"

"I don't know." She pauses, and breathes. She switches course. "But it's not good that you give him everything. Or that you think you give him everything. It doesn't make you a good person."

I don't know why, but I convince myself she means that I've given *her* to Demetri when I shouldn't have. "It was you who left my apartment, Nati. And then I wasn't going to interfere."

She doesn't answer this. Still, we don't hang up.

At last I tell her that it has always been this way: "He set us free from everything," I say. "When we were children. He was being suffocated. And then he set himself free. I don't even know if he meant to. But he made a decision, he set us free, and it's what has allowed us to become everything."

She jumps on this: "But you haven't let him become anything."

"You just said I've given him everything."

"But that's prevented him from so much. Ava." She must be pressing her mouth against the phone. I lean back. "He is always guilty," she continues. "He is always guilty, I think, and has no trust in his impressions. It's why he relies on factual things. His guilt . . ."

I tell her not to talk about his guilt.

"Why is it? He's replaying boyhood? What is it? I don't understand it."

"He's not guilty," I say, holding my throat.

"You two . . ." She pauses. "You know, he hates you, I think, in certain ways. He said so. He hates you." I imagine her cupping her hair behind her ears. "He wonders if you're killing him, if you've killed him."

"No he doesn't."

She waits. "Well then, I wonder."

WHEN I FINALLY hang up, it's to answer the call from a doctor. Demetri, that morning, had nearly slipped into unconsciousness. But he's back now, the doctor tells me. Stable, in deep sleep.

Five days pass. Demetri spends eighteen hours a day with his eyes closed. The nurses call him the Kitty. I come to memorize the carpet in the makeshift sickroom: I notice where it is most red and plush, where it is already thinning, and then lie down upon it and stare up at the wood ceiling.

Mostly I'm out of memory. It's a wire I can no longer pull at. This brings me peace. But then on my seventh consecutive night, two new visions cord through. Demetri and I are standing in the second aisle of Home Depot. Pus is seeping out of his new tattoo. "I need beautiful wood ceilings," he's telling me. It's five years ago and I'm happy: I love the muted cohesion and density of a hardware store, the rows of coils, bristles, plastics, felts, wires, steels. Demetri's fingering cans of Raid and wood polish as we walk through the aisles. "I need wood ceilings and a big tattoo. I'll be serious, but experimental. Classic and formal, but also free-spirited . . ."

I take a sip of the store's free coffee (Demetri has already had two cups) and ask him if he knows how calculated that sounds.

"The world is composed of complex calculations. I treat myself self-similarly."

"That is a fucking absurd thing to say out loud, Demetri."

"I'm not saying it out loud. I'm saying it to you."

We pass the extension cords, outlet covers for children.

Finally the wood samples. As we consider the little sample slabs, a woman turns into our aisle. She's arguing with her son, maybe a first grader. As they come closer I peer down Demi's leg. "You're bleeding," I tell him. We've come directly from the tattoo parlor. He had chosen one of the flash designs—a Hawaiian woman with her arms over her head.

"Don't worry," he says. "I mean it's not just blood that's coming out."

I bend down to look close. "You're leaking ink and pus and blood."

"It's healing!"

"Excuse us," the woman says.

Her son, tombstone height, grunts. I notice he is flooded with that residual anger that children wear so well. I wonder what has happened to him (A bad soccer game? The refusal of a snack? A vague apprehension of death?). The boy looks at Demetri, declares him an enemy, and kicks, slamming his foot into Demetri's leg.

"Jesus fucking—" Demetri stumbles,* puts his weight against the shelf. The square wood samples fall off their displays. The woman pulls her son by the arm. Instead of making him apologize she reprimands him publicly in the next aisle.

"Do you think it's okay?" I mean his tattoo, which will thereafter be smudged.

"What? That children love . . ." He bites his lip. "That they have a bad day and then they see me and they come for me. They know." We lift the samples off the floor and place them back on their display. "They just know something I don't, something very bad about me, and they act accordingly." He's breathing heavily. I look down at his

---

**Stumbles*, watercolor on rice paper, medium
I really did try to get these pigments to stumble onto the paper, just by turning my head away and letting them drip.

leg—now leaking mostly blood—and I bend to lift the last sample off the ground. It's dark oak. I hold it out for us to see. Demetri runs his finger across it.

And so it's dark oak above me.

As I lie on his carpet, I hear him breathing, the monitor going. I try to stand up but my limbs are weighted on the floor.

Soon, the room is black and I don't know what time it is. Again my eyes close.

"I want the floor to be on the ceiling," our mother says. Demetri and I arrive home to find the house disassembled. All the furniture has been moved into the hall, the carpets rolled up.

Now on the floor—in place of the rugs—are huge swaths of crepe paper, the type doctors use to cover medical chairs; fragile paper that rustles and tears at gestures light as breath.

Our mother is holding a small bowl, which contains thick rods of graphite.

"I want the floor on the ceiling," she says again. She is focused. Hard, yellow eyes. Her bare shoulders like soft bulbs of light.

"I want wood-board ceilings. Your father says we can't afford them. We'll do something called rubbing. We will trace and copy the wooden floors and put them up there."

Demetri and I look up to the ceiling and see long strips of double-sided tape, where she intends to stick the paper.

Our mother gets on her knees and begins to rub the graphite over the paper—she begins transferring the patterns from the wood underneath, catching all the small knots and striations.

Demetri and I bend down beside her and do the same. His paper never rips. Mine does. I try to choose the smoothest boards, but the paper will not hold. I ruin so much paper so quickly that my mother exiles me from the project, and she and Demetri continue.

With both of them bent over, I can see the angles of their bodies: from thigh to shin, chest across to bicep; the way their spines curve, the mild slope of their upper scalps. Demetri looks as if he can be folded* right back into her.

When I run and push him over, onto the paper and into our mother, neither of them move. I leave the room.

The reproduced floor stays up for three days. Then the humidity gets to the tape. Our mother lets paper fall piece by piece onto the floor. She doesn't clean up the mess.

SOON, ON THE CARPET of Demetri's sickroom, I wake again, feeling as if that same paper has fallen over my body, as if it's tight over my mouth. I wonder then if I've spent my life drawing and painting not to control paper, or images,

---

**Folded*, acrylic on canvas, medium

or people, or things, but to keep it all away from me, at a remove, to stop the sense of smother.

Demetri is asleep. I close my eyes and do not dream.

THE CARPET IS WARM on my feet when I finally stand up. The lights are on and Demetri is awake. I wipe my eyes and mouth with my arm.

"Hi," I say. I can no longer tell when he's smiling at me.

"Ave." His indigo skin has grown lighter. "It's a little rude just to look at someone . . . and cry."

I laugh. "It's drool. I was sleeping."

"Are you hungry?" There's too much breath in his voice. I have to deflate each sound to parse where one word starts and another ends.

"Yes."

He is silent. I think he will go back to sleep and I feel a surge of anger. But he goes on looking as if he's about to speak. I think he is going to tell me I can't possibly be hungry. Or that I must be hungry. Or that I am never hungry. Or that I am always hungry. Any one of those I would have taken as an absolute truth, as an annunciation on the state of my soul. Instead he moves his body farther up the bed, so his head is at the top of the pillow, and his eyes meet mine. I know he knows.

"You can't tell someone not to have my child, you

know." The unrolling of my interior. I wait. "You can't exactly do that."

There is the hum of the monitor, then its brief pause, then its hum again.

"Am I speaking too softly?"

"No."

"Well?"

Thinking of Nati without thinking she betrayed me. Thinking of Nati and thinking I'd have done the same. Thinking I'm grateful because it does not seem like she's told him everything.

"Don't worry. We're not going to fight," he says.

"You don't have time."

"That's true." He shifts his weight around. "And since I don't have the time, and since I can't leave, you're going to have to leave."

"How do you mean?"

Demetri either sighs or simply breathes. "I mean you're going to have to leave this room."

"For how long?"

"However long it takes."

"However long what takes?" And then, instead of repeating that there is no time for that kind of thing, I say okay, but tell him I have something to forgive him for, too.

"What?"

I want to tell him I of course know he is behind this

Liam Lesser documentary. Word had gotten around, James had emailed me, suspicious after overhearing gossip. Demetri's moves were so banal and clumsy. They were boyish. I held no anger. In California he'd collected our father's tapes. I'm sure he plans to use them. I know he interviewed former classmates. People I never speak to. He must've asked them for cooperation in keeping things hushed. I imagine their agreement, their excitement to take part, all their lingering respect for him. I want to tell him that he is about to embarrass himself, and me, in making whatever he's making. And I want to mention that in essence I know that he betrayed me and that I have kept it to myself. I want to be very proud of this—my maturity. But instead I say never mind.

"Well, say it." He lifts his palm. "It would offend me if you left quietly."

"There's really nothing."

He shakes his head.

"Well," and then my mouth moves without me: "I'm maybe wondering if you perhaps think this child would be some kind of extension of you. Or if you hope it would be an extension of you. Another you. Because this would be bad. Another you would be the imitation of an imitation. A replica of someone who can't stop replicating."

He nods: "Good. Okay. Sounds right. And what am I myself imitating? What am I always replicating?"

"Your first love."

"And what was my first love?"

"Your youth."

This is meant to offend him. It is supposed to be a grand statement about his life, meant to suggest that for all his promise he never did find focus. That he is in constant and confining rehearsal. I want to hurt him because he is leaving me. I want to make him realize he needs more time—to force him back into existence through an acute sense of pain. You're so weak, I want to say. You freed yourself, and it was the last glorious thing you've ever done, and you can't get over how horrific it made you feel, and—because it was an instinct—now you're anti-instinct. Even when you create you are only moving backward. And now you've been so weak your whole life and now you are dying. And I hate you. And I don't understand. And you have let me be generous to you, which is to say you have let me exercise control. An incomplete control, which is the most agonizing, because for instance I cannot control what is happening to you now, and if I try to pull you off this bed you will die, and if I leave you in this bed you will die. And it's unfair because your control over *me* is complete. Because I reach into myself and I find you—and then I move you around to find me and I still find you. And if all of existence in myself is you—this means soon I'll no longer have myself. You are making me hate you.

Demetri laughs. "That's probably true." He closes his eyes. "Okay. Come tomorrow morning," he says. He takes his hands off his lap and lays them by his sides and begins to close his eyes. "It's a formality. When I close my eyes I actually won't even know that you're gone. In the morning I wake up and it's like you never left." I try to smell his breath. "But Ava, you cannot sleep here. You have to go."

"So the punishment is just for me?"

"Who else would it be for?" Here he really laughs. His eyes are still closed. He tells me I need real sleep. Not just red-carpet sleep. I nod, but he can't see me. I am about to say fine. He clears his throat. "Plus, Ava, you look like you're dying."

I stand there until I hear him begin to snore, and then leave before Nati arrives.

I'm not thinking.

I GO HOME to find my portraits of her, choose one where she's leaning forward, and bring it to him at night.

He is awake when I enter his room and bring it out. (Though here I will admit that for a split second, on entering, I thought he was dead. It was the stillness in his eyes. I gathered myself.)

"Look what I did," I say.

I watch him. I hold the portrait up for him. I want him to make me leave before he sees anything. I swallow and oppress the feeling. "Is this right?" I ask him. I point to her spine.

Demetri doesn't answer. I can't tell if his eyes are open. He can't hold the canvas himself, so I continue to support it for him.

"And I have more," I say.

After a moment he is still silent.

I ask him again if it's right. I see he is staring at the colors. "Demetri, can you tell me, please . . ."

I notice, looking close, that his eyes are beginning to rove. This has happened before. His eyes turn in a slow, methodical movement that I know he can't control. I stand still and watch him until, in some kind of prismatic shift, like someone's pinched the center plane of reality and tilted it, I feel myself seized, caught and unable to speak, my shoulders heaved up, because shaken loose from the back of Demetri's skull, back where they'd imprinted themselves, are my mother and father, wheeling in and out of his eyes.

I feel panic.

At last his eyes stop roving. There is control, they are aware.

First they move up over the crown of my head, down again, and finally they meet me. The look is empty. He is absent inside of it. But it holds.*

**Holds*, soot on canvas, extra large
The candle from the back of the silverware drawer.
How to get at anything that is empty, but holding.

IN THE SILENCE I fall asleep on the floor beneath him.

And deep into the night, with a sound as soft as breath ceasing, my brother's brain stem torques, twists inward, forever isolates him into a deeper shade.

I GO HOME and immediately begin to paint him.

I work in no order.

Nine months later. He has not woken up.

Of course, the world shuts down.

I do not talk to Nati. Or rather she will not talk to me. Finding the portrait in Demetri's room, she cannot find words for me. She can't understand it—that he needed one last beautiful thing, to be moved once more. If he was going away, beauty—or the purity of hatred, some kind of obliteration—was what should take him there.

Last month Nati gave birth to a boy, Arion.

And then, because misery loves momentum, two weeks after Arion's birth Nati's mother died. She is now in Italy but was not allowed to take infant Arion. He is so light he cannot fly. And so he is with me. Dropped off with a crib, stroller, playpen, all the instruments, and a binder of written instructions.

I pray Nati will not come back.

I have reason to believe she won't. Despite her organized delivery of everything Arion, she gave him over too willingly, as if releasing him was releasing death and grief, giving them to me.

Good. Baby baby.

Sometimes he smiles, but at almost all moments he cries, with his puffy skin swollen hard.

Sometimes I put my finger in front of him so that he will grasp it. I remember he has no choice but to do so, that it is a reflex, that his mind and body are simply preparing him to reach for things. Sometimes I feel accused in the way he looks at me. As if he's already asking me what I've done to him. And sometimes his rheumy eyes age him, and I can relax, convinced he is blind.

This morning the phone keeps ringing. In two hours the Withheld assistant will knock once more. I won't answer. I am still in my kitchen, where Demetri is alive and pulsing with color. He wanted a single idea—developed and evolved—it's there in what I've made of him. An ethics of ecstatic flashes. An ethics of exposure. And in this writing: the catalog—the written accompaniment—everything Demetri could not say. There will be more shows to come. A show of Nati, maybe, for when I really feel like losing everything.

Just now, in breaks from my writing, I've been leaning the final pieces against the wall. I'm thinking of the film Demetri has made of us. It's getting attention. It's winning prizes. It's been selected for two festivals. It's airing tonight somewhere in an elegantly produced room, being put before more judges and juries. People send me messages, there are little posts about it—everyone who hasn't seen it is excited to preemptively praise it. I am told there is a scene of me painting, my back to the camera, and that Demetri has put this in slow motion: I hold my paintbrush, my arm lifts, I run the brush across the canvas. You can see the effect of each long stroke. You can see my back contort. And I'm realizing now that if you watch what Demetri has made, you might see me in a café and you might, in fact, know me from behind.

Right now I have to go to Arion. He's laughing in his crib.

He's always laughing. Even when he dreams, he laughs.

What jokes are you telling yourself? I want to ask him.

This is what I'll do: I will walk toward his crib. He will be asleep. I will listen to his silence. And then I will hear it—a kind of patterned hiccup. I will watch him twitch for a moment, in the throes of his dream, and then I will wake him up. He won't mind. He will look up at me. His eyes will be alien. They will be blue and green and gray and brown; they will be clay and mud. I will look at him and wonder what palette I'll use for his blotched skin, for his loose tuft of hair, his meat-locker complexion.

"Hi," I will say to him.

His eyes will squint at me, without recognition or expectation.

I will put out my finger, right in front of his hand, and I

will make him cling to me. He will, and then he'll let go. I'll put out my finger again. He'll cling to it again, then shake me. Not off, just hard.

This baby, by the way, looks like nobody. Or, he looks like every other baby. He cries like every other baby. He has no history, he has no habits, and so he is unknowable. But he is visual. He is an image, and he will develop.

I will make him into something.

ACKNOWLEDGMENTS

I would like to thank and acknowledge my entire wild family, including Beckett and Madonna. I would like to thank my agent, Susan, and her assistant, Sasha. I would like to thank Troy. I would like to thank Ioanna (and baby Eva). Also Sam, Gary, and Rivka, for reading this in one of its ugliest forms. I would like to thank the late Kirk Varnedoe and Peter Schjeldahl. The biggest thank-you to Penguin Press, specifically my editor, Casey Denis, for not only her faith and brilliance but also her inimitable charisma. I would like to thank New York City and every tiny gallery and large museum therein. And, lastly, I would like to thank Joseph, without whom nothing would be possible.